AT WEEK'S END

SHERELLE WINTERS

This story and the characters within it are fictional. However, the forest of Aokigahara and the towns mentioned in this story are all quite real. There are also references to historical events as well as Japanese cultural views.

I've tried to describe these ideas, areas, and the forest itself as accurately as possible, though occasionally I fudged a bit to fit the story's needs. Any errors found, particularly regarding geography or cultural norms, are either a result of this creative expression or an error in my research.

For permission requests, contact the publisher:

Zenbi Press
1511 Texas Avenue S #325
College Station, Texas 77840-3328

Cover Design: Kerry Jesberger, Aero Gallerie (http://aerogallerie.com/)

ISBNs
    978-1-949055-06-1 (pbk)
    978-1-949055-07-8 (hdbk)
    978-1-949055-08-5 (ebook)

Library of Congress Control Number: 2018905594

First Printed 2018

Into the Forest

FLYING WOULD HAVE BEEN faster, maybe even cheaper by the time you factored in the gas and wear on the car, but I wanted to drive there, the same as they had. What had the trip been like, driving six hours with your family, knowing you would die at your destination? Had it been a solemn drive, with the kids nodding off in the back and the adults not speaking? Or had the parents made it feel like a family trip, with singing and chattering and all, not wanting the kids to know the truth of what was to come.

My trip started at my low-rent, slightly above dive-level apartment in Osaka. It was a ridiculously early hour even for me. The sun was at least an hour from rising when I slipped on my jacket, threw my backpack over my shoulder, grabbed my coffee, and headed out the door. As I turned the key in the lock, I placed my palm against the door a moment. I'd lived there a good six years now, it was home. Despite having visited a wide range of hotels over the last few years, I never found one where I slept as well as I did on my cheap futon at home.

It was a long drive, with only one pause to refill the tank. The sun rose as I drove, but it barely registered in my mind. In truth, I remembered little of the drive, and it may well be a miracle I even made it to my destination in one piece. For my mind was on them, the Nakamura family, the family I'd murdered, the family whose death site I was making this pilgrimage to see.

I'm not even sure what compelled me to make this journey, beyond some vague need to go there now, and that when I arrived there was something I had to do. The idea first came to me after one of my many failed attempts at drowning out the memories in a bottle of shōchū. Unlike the many other similar ideas of restitution that had come to me during my drunken crying spells, this one stuck around after I was relatively sober again.

Even as the wheels ate up the kilometers, I could not figure out why I was going, what purpose this visit would serve. Only that going no longer felt like an option. Hell, it wasn't as if I had anything else to do anyway, beyond make a pest of myself to one of the few friends I had left, or worrying him and his family with the drinking. He and his family had gone back to Hokkaido to visit relatives this week, which was good. I couldn't even phantom how much more they would worry if they knew where I was heading.

Shortly before noon, I pulled into the parking lot at the northern entrance of Aokigahara, near the Narusawa Ice

Cave. It was almost surreal in its normalcy. Half a dozen cars dotted the parking lot, along with a tour bus. The visitor's center noted guided tours of the forest were available for a small fee and had a gift shop featuring local wares. There was even a small ice cream shop. Had I been here for a story, it would have been a pleasant start to the visit. Before the Nakamuras, I might have even stopped there and thought of writing a story to help combat its morbid reputation.

But today, the verdant forest stretched before me did not inspire awe; rather it was foreboding, shaded in darkness and misery despite the sun blazing overhead. I could almost hear their voices, just as I had so many times in my nightmares, whispering, beckoning me to continue the journey I'd started. As much as I wanted to turn around and go home, I owed it to them to go to their final resting spot, the scene of the crime.

After forcing myself to get out of the car, I retrieved my backpack and a bottle of water to tuck into its side pouch. I picked up my cell phone from the console but stopped myself from pocketing it. It wasn't anything I needed today, and the last thing I wanted was to be at that sacred spot and get another call about what a monster I was, so I tossed it in the glove box before locking the car.

I'd managed to time my arrival so that no other visitors entered at the same time or were even within view. As I had no need of a map, and I had no desire to converse with anyone, I bypassed the visitor's center. Still, walking past, I returned the wary greeting from the employee outside sweeping with a wave and what I hoped passed for a cheerful smile. I didn't need them thinking I was one of their less desired visitors and feel they needed to come stage an intervention or something.

Near the entrance was a large sign, dark brown with bright white writing. I'd heard they were at every entrance and at regular spots along the trail.

> **PLEASE THINK ONCE MORE ABOUT THE PRECIOUS LIFE GIVEN TO YOU BY YOUR PARENTS.**
>
> **THINK ABOUT YOUR FAMILY, YOUR FRIENDS.**
>
> **YOU DON'T HAVE TO SUFFER ALONE.**

At the bottom was the number for the local police station. For the first time in days I felt something other than numbing apathy. Anger boiled inside me as I read those words: "the precious life given to you by your parents." I pulled the article and photo that had taken permanent residence on my person out of my pocket and held it up. The Nakamura family stared back at me, their eyes accusing as always. This time, I focused on the children.

The quiet, studious girl of twelve, who'd been considered a promising young singer. The seven-year-old boy, grinning despite his pallor. Even towards the end, it was said he kept a cheerful disposition, comforting his parents and sister rather than focusing on his own struggles. Mature beyond his age. Had he lived, he would no doubt have grown to be a good man, respectable and well-liked by many.

Had those two children, not even close to being adults, been given the chance to think about their precious lives?

As they walked passed this very same sign, perhaps each holding one of their parents' hands, had they known they would never leave? Did Takuji and his wife give them a choice in drinking the poisoned water, or had their last gift to their children been the blessing of ignorance? Had they lied and said they were just taking a short rest break, gently encouraging them to nap when they started yawning, and letting the children drift off without ever telling them they would never wake up?

A heavy sigh escaped my lips, taking the flash of anger with it. It didn't matter who did the actual deed; in the end the fault was mine. I was the one responsible for their deaths. I cost the world those lovely children as sure as if I'd shoved the poison in their throats myself. And now it was time to atone for my sins.

Before my cowardice could make me go back to hiding from the truth, I started down the wide dirt trail that formed the most visible human mark on the place beyond the signs. It was easy to see why there were so many warnings about staying on the path. Even for the many visitors who came to the forest with no intention of taking their own life, straying from the marked areas could well lead to death simply by being unable to find your way out again before thirst, hunger, the elements, or all three combined to finish you off. At best, I could see maybe two or three meters into the brush, sometimes not even that. And while the path itself was clear, the trees had grown in overhead, as if determined to reclaim even this small bit of itself from the paltry human interlopers that dared to walk through it.

Though I knew it was entirely natural, the quietness didn't feel like it. There was almost no noise. No birds, no calls of little creatures moving around. I'd been expecting it of course, from reading about the forest after the Nakamuras' deaths, but still, part of me hadn't believed that the trees could be so dense that there would be almost no wind. Or the ground so hard from being mostly made of volcanic rock that it supported little animal life. The combination of deathly quiet and brilliantly alive fauna was unnerving, and yet again I found myself wanting to turn and forgo my mission.

Instead, I paused and retrieved the map from my backpack, the task of finding where to turn off giving me something else to focus on. Thanks to a disgusted but well paid contact, I secured a good map of the forest marking where the Nakamura family had been found during one of the regular sweeps for the bodies of those who'd succeeded in their attempt to die by suicide. The local government no longer indicated how many bodies they found, or how many the rangers and volunteers had been able to save. But they still took notes on every location, so that the loved ones left behind could visit those spots, if desired, to leave memorials.

Of course, most families were escorted by one of the park officials who could ensure they did not get lost or decide to follow their loved ones into the afterlife. But I was on my own, the contact not willing to go that far for me. When we'd met to exchange the map for my funds, the man made it clear that he'd only done this much due to Shinji's influence and that he considered me scum. He'd been with the team who found the family, mother and father lying together with the children snuggled between them as if they were a happy family napping in a cool, quiet spot. While the sweeper teams had a high turnover rate due to the sheer stress and heartache of the job, seeing those young kids had been the worst, and I was told in a biting voice how three of their employees had quit that very day, unable to take it anymore.

Checking the map one last time, I soldiered on, refusing to look at anything other than the path ahead for fear of finding something I didn't want to see. I was told the spot was about eight kilometers in and should only take me a few hours to reach. I didn't see how it would even take that long, at least not until I reached the place about three kilometers in where the map indicated I needed to go off path and head east. Glancing at the forest in front of me, I had a feeling I was about to find out where the rest of that time was coming from.

Even in my state, I couldn't help noticing the irony of my going off path by stepping over one of the very chains intended to discourage just such a thing. I also ignored the sensible suggestion I'd read in my research to mark the trees with reflective tape, so I could easily find my way out again. After all, I had the map, plus a good compass, and I knew how to use both. Why litter up the trees, or leave a mess behind that I'd just have to pick up on my way out?

The gnarled roots of the forest's inhabitants crawled along the ground, unable to penetrate the thick rock that lay just below the shallow layer of soil. One would think such a place would have little plant life, but instead it thrived, I presumed due to the incredible richness of the soil. The thick moss that covered nearly everything in sight, and the humidity had me panting even in the relatively cool temperatures.

As I stumbled and faltered along the hilly terrain, I laughed in self-derision at my foolish idea that my school trips to the woods had prepared me adequately for this journey. Even more than it had on the path, the overhead canopy blocked a surprising amount of the sun. I knew it was right overhead, but even its warm rays could not penetrate the underlying darkness of the place. I debated using my flashlight, but I hadn't brought any spare batteries and the time it was taking me to move forward left me concerned I'd be having to make my way back out later in the day than planned. As long as there was enough light to check my compass and map every few meters to confirm I was mostly going in the right direction, I could deal with the rest.

I was perhaps halfway to my destination when I found a small clearing that was a little better lit thanks to a break in the canopy above. The small path of light led down to a girl sitting on the trunk of a fallen tree that lay across the opening. The angle of the log and the way she was facing kept her from seeing me, though I was surprised she hadn't heard me approach.

Long, wine red hair ran halfway down her back, the color a startling contrast to the light sweater covering her slender frame. Jeans protected her legs from the underbrush that she would have had to go through to get here, the same as I had, and she wore sensible boots like any regular visitor. But why would a visitor be so far off the path?

Then I spotted the bottle of pills in one hand and a bottle of water in the other.

"Good afternoon." My voice seemed obscenely loud as I stepped into the clearing so she could see me.

She turned slowly and looked at me, her head tilted slightly to the side. I had expected her to look startled or maybe even guilty at being caught, but instead she just regarded me with a vaguely curious expression. From the back, I'd taken her to be a teenager, but seeing her face now, I adjusted my estimate to early twenties, the same age as me, or maybe just a little younger.

"Hi." A smile flashed across her pink-tinted lips. It threw me off balance. Surely someone about to die wouldn't look at me like that? Maybe she just had a headache and had stopped to rest, same as I'd considered.

I stayed at a respectable distance, not wanting to frighten her. Three months of barely sleeping, of dealing with interviews and accusations, the haunting images of the Nakamura children, and more alcohol than I could remember hadn't left me looking like a nice guy. I hadn't bothered to shave in a while, and a quick glance down confirmed my clothes were wrinkled and of questionable cleanliness. I no doubt looked like a bum, and as if I was the one there to end his life, not the other way around.

"Did you want to use this spot too?" Her question quickly dispelled my hopes she was just a wandering tourist.

"Um, no, just passing through."

"Oh, okay." Another quick smile. She had a pretty smile, friendly and generous. I vaguely thought that in some other setting, she would be the sort of girl to light up a room with her cheerful nature.

"Are you… I mean…" I made a vague motion towards her hands.

If anything, her smile was brighter this time, and she even laughed, a sweet sound so at odds with what came next. "Why else would I be here? I mean, it is kinda cool walking around here, but it isn't the sort of place anyone would come to camp out just for fun."

I'd done a piece on the rate of suicides in Japan, but at that moment, I couldn't remember a single bit about how to stop someone who was contemplating it. I hadn't come here to find someone else who came to die; I'd come to find the spot they already had. But even in my self-loathing, I couldn't make myself walk away. "Mind if I sit down a minute? It's more humid here than I expected and it's left me a little tired."

"Sure, go ahead. Want some water?" She offered up the bottle in her hand.

"Thanks, but I have some." I sat on the same fallen tree, being careful to stay a meter or so away as I pulled out my water and took a sip. Until I felt the water on my tongue, I hadn't realized I actually was thirsty. I took a few swallows, watching her watch me over the bottle. Could she tell I was freaking out, trying to figure out what to say? "So, um, what's your name?"

"You can call me Yuna. What about you?"

"Adachi. Tsuguru Adachi." I braced myself, half expecting some outraged response, some instant recognition of my name that would cause her to hate me too.

"Pleased to meet you, Adachi." She'd managed to throw me off again, saying my first name without any honorific. I also realized she hadn't given me her family name, but before I could ask, she spoke again. "Did you come here to die too?"

"Ah, no, I, uh, I just wanted to see the famous forest."

"Yeah right. Even the macabre ones don't come this far off the paths unless they are following someone's death lines. And the regular tourists are far too afraid of the ghosts and goblins." She raised her hands up with her fingers hooked like a kid telling a scary story around a camp fire. "You don't look like you're just hunting for someone's body to exploit for some stupid video on-line, and you don't have that scared look of someone who wandered too far and got lost."

"Ah. True. It's rough going and a bit unnerving, but not horrible. I'd probably be terrified to be here at night though. With all the stories about hauntings and stuff, I wouldn't be surprised if there is at least a little truth to them."

She unscrewed the cap off the water bottle in her hand and took a few swallows, then carefully returned the cap. The motions allowed me to get a better view of the bottle her in her hand, a prescription sleeping pill. If I could take the bottle from her, then she'd have to give up right? Then I spotted a large backpack on the other side of the log near her legs. What all did she have in there; more tools for dying?

"You can't stop me, you know." She said it as casually as if she were telling me the time, even flashed me another of those brilliant smiles. She really did seem to smile an awful lot for someone who was suicidal. Indeed, nothing in her demeanor or appearance gave any hints of desperation or despondency. In any other place, I'd have thought she was just a young woman out enjoying the woods.

Unsure how else to respond, I asked the first question that came to mind when I'd realized what she was doing. "Why?"

"Because I've made up my mind. Even if you take my pills or managed to steal my bag, I'll just find another way. If I had to, there are plenty of sharp bits of rock around I could use to slit my wrists and throat."

A shudder ran through me at that image. "No, no, I meant, um… why do you want to die?"

"Oh." Another laugh. "Because I'm done with living. I've lived all I wish to, so I figured I might as well go now."

"But you're so young! I mean, you're what, 22, 23? There is so much more left to life yet!"

"I'm 22, since you asked." She didn't ask my age, so I didn't tell her I was only three years older than her. I probably looked much older right then.

She hadn't responded to the second part of my statement, so I tried another tactic. "Look, I'm not going to say I'm the best listener in the world or anything, but since I'm here, why not talk to me about it anyway? Maybe it would help."

"Talk to you about what?"

"Well, whatever has you depressed."

Again she laughed. "I'm not depressed. I'm simply done with living, like I said. There is nothing left that I wish to do or experience, so why stick around spending years living some boring, meaningless existence that really would make me depressed?"

"But, how do you know that? I mean you haven't married yet, right? Or had kids? What about a career? You're probably just out of college, so surely there are a lot of interesting things left yet to see and do?"

This time she didn't laugh, just turned up the corners of her lips a little with an expression that looked as if she pitied me. "So you want a wife and kids, huh?"

"Well, I guess, yeah. At least, I always thought I would."

"Hmmm, do you have a girlfriend?"

"No… not at the moment." Hiyori dumped me after

I'd told her about the Nakamuras. Before she'd left, she told me I was a disgusting jerk, a fool so blinded by his own ambition that he'd destroyed others in the process and cost an innocent family their lives.

"What about a career? What do you do?"

"I'm a reporter, or at least I was…" I let my voice trail off. When I tried to quit, my boss refused to accept it, instead encouraging me to take some time to recover before deciding. Had he turned his back on me too, it would have been easier, but even though he'd had to bow his head for my screw up so many times, he was still offering me a chance. That had kept me from just walking away entirely, but I couldn't see myself going back, not after having betrayed my own ethical compass so badly.

"A reporter?" She sat up a little straighter, her sharp gaze raking over me in fresh assessment. "Like for TV?"

"Ah, no, newspaper."

"Even better, they actually still report stuff." Another smile; I'd lost count. "So, are you here for a story then?"

"No, no, just on vacation."

"Oh." She stood and dusted off her pants legs. "Well, it was nice to meet you, Adachi, but I should get going, things to do and all." She shook the pill bottle at me before stuffing it in her pocket.

Even with that signature smile, the dismissal was clear in her voice. She was ready to continue with her death. I'd hoped maybe just talking to her a bit would give her time to think, but clearly not.

"But what about your family? They will be terribly hurt if you do this."

"Don't have any, thanks. And no friends either before you try that one. It's just me, and I'm fine with being gone."

"Isn't there any way I can change your mind? I'm sure if you just wait a few days, things will look better and you'll find a new reason to live."

"I've planned this for weeks, so I doubt a few more days would change my mind." She picked up the backpack, carefully positioning it on her back. It looked heavy, the kind campers used. With a half-smile and a wave, she started walking away.

"Please, Yuna-chan, please, wait!" I wanted to jump up and grab her arm to hold her there, but I was paralyzed with the fear that I was somehow causing yet another person's death. My voice broke as I called out again. "Please, don't go yet!"

She stopped moving. "Do you really want to stop me that much? Why do you care one way or another?"

"I just… I have too much blood on my hands already. I don't need anymore."

She looked back at me, her face more serious than it had been during the entirety of our encounter so far. It felt almost as if she were trying to read my very soul. We stayed like that for a full minute, her standing across the clearing watching me, me sitting on that log barely breathing out of fear that any movement would break the spell and she'd leave. By the time I could summon help, she'd be long gone and it might take weeks, even months to find her body as she too had no markers showing her path.

Finally, an enigmatic smile appeared on her lips. "Okay, Adachi, if you feel that strongly about that, I'll wait…"

"Really?" Relief coursed through me, until she finished her statement.

"…but only for one week, and only if you agree to stay with me for the entire time."

"What do you mean stay with you?"

"Just that. You'll spend the next seven days with me, and we'll wander around this place together. Then, at the end of the week, next Saturday at," she paused to check her watch, "2:47 p.m., if I've changed my mind I'll leave. We can even walk out together if you like. But, if I haven't, then you'll let me die in peace."

Seven days in this forest with her? Sleeping in this haunted, death filled place? "I…"

"What do you say?"

"What will we do about food? We can't go that long without eating."

"I have some retort meals and other stuff in my bag. Should be enough to last awhile. You probably have something in your bag too, right?"

"A little, yes, though not a week's worth."

She shrugged. "We'll make do. Oh, and if you leave my sight for more than two minutes, then the deal is off. So, what do you say?"

Not willing to risk losing the small opening she'd given me, I stood and closed the distance between us. Grabbing her hand in a firm shake, I grimly agreed. "Fine, it's a deal."

The First Day

Present

AFTER I RETRIEVED MY backpack, I followed her into the forest without a word. A quick glance at my compass showed we were now going in a southeastern direction, away from the Nakamuras' final spot. I didn't complain though; it wasn't something I wanted to have to explain, much less a place I wanted to visit while accompanied by a stranger. Going was hard enough as it was.

We walked along in silence for a while. If Yuna had any particular destination in mind, I couldn't tell. She seemed to meander around, pausing frequently to look at the unusual root structures, the trees, all the little caves and holes that only made the terrain treacherous. Despite not checking any guide tool that I could see, she didn't seem to have a care in the world. If I hadn't known better, I'd have thought her a regular girl enjoying a hike through the forest.

The silence stretched longer, other than the random noises she'd sometimes make while looking into the caves. For some, she pulled the flashlight from her belt to look inside better. As I trudged along behind her, I tried to think of what to say or do now. I'd made the deal out of desperation, anything to buy some time to get her to rethink her views on life. But afterwards I was mentally floundering trying to come up with said magic trick.

Finally, needing to hear something in that preternatural silence I decided to make small talk, get to know her and maybe gain the knowledge I needed to help her want to live. "That backpack…" I started at the sound of my own voice, almost obscene in its volume. When I continued, I lowered my tone, even though it was unlikely I was bothering a soul. "It looks like the sort a camper might use?"

"Yep, it is. I got into hiking and stuff, so I got a good bag to let me carry my own gear instead of having to rent all the time." Her statement was punctuated with a grin. "And before you ask, yes, I have supplies for an overnight stay. A tent, a sleeping bag, and the food. When I came, I'd considered that it might take me awhile to find a suitable spot."

"Oh… so that clearing was one?"

"No, not really. I'd already been thinking I wasn't feeling that spot when you came along. If you'd been five minutes later, I'd have probably already left and we wouldn't have run into each other."

"I see…well, then I'm glad I wasn't running late." I tried to smile at her, but I was torn between annoyance and fear. Annoyance at her selfishness in blackmailing me to stay with her, versus just being willing to go home and think for a week about what she'd been planning. What purpose was there in her forcing me to be her hostage for a week? And what if at the end of the week, she still felt the same? Or worse, I only made her even more determined! Would I be forced to sit and watch her die? Somehow, I had to change her mind; even it meant playing companion for a while.

"Hey, Adachi, what kind of reporting do you do at your paper?" She paused to let me come up beside her.

"What do you mean?"

"Well, do you write for the sports section, lifestyle, local news, you know that kinda thing?"

"Oh, um, I'm assigned to the business and finance section right now."

"Darn, I don't read those sections much, so I guess I wouldn't have seen any of your stories. Sorry."

I shrugged in self-deprecation. "It's okay, it's all pretty dry reading unless you're a business manager or into investing and stuff."

After a negligent glance around us, she continued walking, but kept the conversation up. "You don't sound like you really enjoy it very much."

"It's okay, I guess. I mean, it is important information for people to know, at least the ones it affects. I must admit, though, it wasn't what I planned to do forever. It was supposed to be a temporary stopping spot to get my real goal." But my attempt to get to that goal faster had backfired big time, not that I was about to tell her that part. "When you first join any kind of news organization you don't have a lot of say in what section you actually work in. We all start at some low-level position, wherever there is a need, and as we show promise we get promoted or passed to other departments. If we're lucky, the manager notices our passion for our goal area and will help us move to it as efficiently as possible."

"Ah, so you're still at the entry level then?"

"Sort of, though it's my second assignment now. I joined the paper three years ago, fresh out of college. Initially I was assigned to the human-interest section."

She nodded for some reason. "I bet you liked that better?"

"Yes, I suppose I did. A lot of them were small tales, things that most people would read for brief entertainment before forgetting it. But they were also fascinating little vignettes into other people's lives and the strange, beautiful world we live in. They were more interesting to research, and I enjoyed distilling them into the final articles more." I paused, feeling self-conscious about how much I was talking, but Yuna gestured for me to continue. "Ah, well, I guess with many of those stories, I felt like I learned more, not just about life in general but often about myself. One story even reconnected me with someone I knew in high school."

"Wow, really? What was it about?"

Again, I found myself hesitating, afraid of sharing too much, but seeing her interest encouraged me to continue. If sharing some of my past helped her find the will to continue living, what did it matter? "I'd been sent to check out a hot new chef who was still getting started running his restaurant, Trio Amoroso, but was already quite popular with the locals. When I arrived to interview him, I was surprised to find he was my former classmate, Shinji.

I had no idea he had even moved to Osaka. Funny thing is, in school we weren't particularly close, barely talked at all really, but after meeting again like that, we've become good friends. We still talk almost every week, and I visited his family not too long ago."

"That is amazing." Her smile was somehow brighter than ever. It was if she had a 1000-watt bulb in her face and kept finding new ways of turning it up. Something about those smiles though, they made me feel almost comforted, as if her smile and happiness were embracing me in a warm blanket. It still made no sense, how someone could smile like that, yet feel she had no reason to live. I just didn't understand how she couldn't see that she seemed perfectly happy, so happy I felt almost jealous of it. Then again, I suppose just a few months ago I looked the same, even as my world was falling apart, before I'd lost the ability to fake it anymore.

"What's another story from then, the one you remember the most?" Her voice broke through the vague idea that had started forming in my head.

"Hmm? Oh, um…let's see. I think it would have to be the Hisakawa family. The matriarch had just turned 100-years-old. A long, happy life, though by itself, not entirely newsworthy. What had caught our eye though was the amazing connection between the generations. It wasn't just her birthday, it was the birthday of all the first-born daughters that were alive. Her daughter had been born on her 25th birthday, her granddaughter came exactly 25 years later, her great-granddaughter 25 years after that, and while we were doing the story, the great-great granddaughter arrived! It was amazing, five generations of women who all had their first daughters on the exact same day at the exact same age. They even had the same hair and eye color, and similar facial structures."

"Seriously? Wow! That's amazing. And they didn't just fake it to make the news or anything?"

I laughed, delighted at her skepticism. So many people just accepted what they were told at face value that her questioning was refreshing. "No, it was all real. I double checked the birth certificates and hospital records just to be sure because it really did seem statistically impossible."

"Did they do a big celebration?"

"Oh yeah, it was huge. And they were all so warm and friendly, they even invited me to join them, wouldn't really take no for an answer. Treated me like one of the family. They had a huge cake, big buffet dinner, relatives from all over. It was a blast, I really enjoyed it there. I came home feeling so alive, I was even singing in the car on the drive back."

Her laugh danced through the trees, a musical sound that made even my withered heart skip a beat. "That sounds like a lot of fun. Did they invite you to the party the next year too?"

"Yes, they did, and every year since. I…" I felt my face fell. "I went that first time, but then I couldn't bring myself to go again."

"Why not?"

When the story had come to mind I'd temporarily forgotten the ending, and I suddenly regretted bringing it up. I debated waving it aside, but her intense gaze had me frozen in place. It felt as if I tried to lie now, any headway I'd made would be lost. Would she consider the deal off if she felt I was hiding things? I wasn't sure, but I didn't want to risk it.

"The second year, the last story I covered before moving to the business section was also about the family. The matron had passed away of a heart attack. It felt almost like losing a member of my own family. She'd… she'd call randomly to check on me since we'd met, really did seem to see me as one of them. Even though I know she lived a good long life, it hurt realizing I'd never hear her cheerful voice on the line again, or laugh at her outrageously bawdy jokes."

Her expression shifted to one of sympathy and a tinge of sadness. She continued walking a bit before speaking again. "Adachi, are you sure being a reporter is the right job for you?"

"What do you mean?" Even I could hear the defensive edge in my voice. Not like I hadn't screwed up, but still, I had a little pride left in my work from before then.

"It seems like the sort of career that would be hard on someone like you. I would say you are a sensitive man with a kind heart. The news is so full of depressing and bad stuff. I would think it would leave you hurting to be around that all the time."

It was true; a lot of the stuff in the news was sad or infuriating. Natural disasters, war, crime, children born with debilitating physical or mental disabilities, accidents. I had good stories I got to report on, but the rest had been draining.

"Maybe. It isn't the first time I've been told that, or that this business would tear me apart. It's part of why I was moved to the business section, I think. But still, I wanted to do this, needed to. I…I wanted to be a truth teller, to bring the real stories, the real truths to people, you know? To tell the public about the things they needed to know to be properly informed and make wise decisions. To help keep our government honest and expose any corruption so that they couldn't misuse their power. I just… I wanted to give the world the truth."

She stopped and leaned against a tree to take a sip of water. When I was even with her, I retrieved my own bottle, mimicking her motions. As I drank, I realized she was watching me. The way she smiled and laughed so freely, I'd taken her to be a bit of an airhead or a flake, but feeling her eyes on me that way, it felt as if she was reading my soul and discerning my every secret. It made me fidget a bit as I returned my bottle to my bag.

"What kind of reporting do you really want to do?" She asked.

Once upon a time, I'd been certain of my answer and could have responded without any thought. But now…yet there she was, those amber eyes watching me, waiting for an answer. I tried to think of something to throw out as a platitude, just something to satisfy her curiosity, but then she shrugged again and pushed herself off the tree while flashing me another smile.

"It's okay. You can tell me later. Come on, let's go this way."

Before I followed her, I checked my compass. At some point we'd turned again. I was certain she didn't know where she was going; she was just following her whims and going wherever her mood struck her. If I hadn't been with her, she would have been hopelessly lost and have likely starved to death, though I guess she didn't really care about that since she'd come there to die.

When I glanced up, she was already several trees away. I'd found out just how serious she was about her rule of being out of sight when she'd watched me from nearby while I'd urinated by a tree and required me to stay in sight while she did the same. I shoved the compass in my bag and raced after her as fast as the thick roots and steadily decreasing visibility would allow. I almost face planted after my foot caught on one such root, but I somehow managed to stay up after a stumbling dance and kept going. I was panting a little as I regained my position less than a foot behind her. Her shoulders shook, making me suspect she was laughing at me.

We walked in silence again for a while. She'd finally stop inspecting the little caves and tree structures, seeming to move with more purpose despite her wandering nature. It was dark enough that I debated taking out my flashlight when she stopped and waited for me to come stand beside her on the edge of a clearing, similar the one where we met. I'd have almost suspected it was the same one except there were no logs in this one and I could hear a stream nearby.

"This looks like a good spot to stop for the night, eh?"

"Um, sure." I shrugged, having no idea what was a good spot or not.

Yuna moved into the clearing, set down her backpack, and pulled a yellow cylindrical sack from the back. I watched in wonder as she expertly pulled a folded set of poles from the bag and got them set up, then attached them to a rectangle of mesh that I realized was the bottom of a tent. I offered to help, but she shook off the offer and said she'd be done in a moment. And she was, moving around so efficiently that I'd have just been in her way if she'd let me "help."

Soon enough, a small but comfortable enough looking

tent was nestled in the center of the clearing. It was a simple, lightweight tent, just tall enough for us to both sit up in comfortably. It wouldn't be much protection from the elements if it got cold, but it would be better than sleeping in the open as the temperature seemed to be dropping by the minute. She removed her shoes and left them upside down near the entrance to the tent, then carried her bag inside.

I presumed her two-minute rule meant I wouldn't be sleeping outside on the ground, so I followed. As I crawled inside, light filled the tent thanks to a short, round lantern now hanging from the top of the tent. She motioned for me to zip the opening closed.

"Did you bring a blanket or anything?"

I shook my head. I'd had no intention of staying longer than I had to.

"I guess we'll just have to share then. Fortunately for you, I like big sleeping bags and I brought my camping gear with me." Her laugh filled the tent as she motioned towards the dark roll lying near her, now detached from the side of her backpack. If nothing else, I was certain that she must have had second thoughts about dying and that her earlier statement of being unable to be stopped had just been bravado. Now I just had to figure out how I could use that uncertainly to get her to change her mind and let us leave, preferably in the morning.

We had another period of silence while we ate the bentos from our respective sacks, each seeming lost in our own thoughts. In my case, it was all in how to convince her, what tactics to use, and trying so hard to remember the bits of information I'd learned during one of my first assignments discussing suicide.

I thought back to the signs at the entrance, but telling her to think about her family was useless. She'd already said she didn't have any or friends. But I wondered if that was really true? She was a pretty girl and, other than wanting to die, seemed to have a fun personality. If it hadn't been for why we were both there, I'd have likely enjoyed talking with her quite a bit. Family could be explained by tragic circumstances, but it was hard to imagine her not having a passel of friends in her life.

I recalled the speech my boss had given me when I'd started at the paper, about the importance of our work and why every story mattered, even if it seemed unimportant. He'd emphasized the need to truly understand the subjects of my story. That their lives and part in the story began long before the part of interest, and that learning about the how and why that got them there, and the person they had been before, would help me find the true story to tell. He would probably tell me that if I wanted to change her mind, I first had to get to know her, to learn what had driven her to this point. The vague idea I'd had earlier returned, becoming more solid as I finished my meal.

"Yuna, while we're here, would you like to tell me your story?" Taking my cue from her, I dropped the honorific from her name.

"So you can do a report on it, you mean?"

"Yes, in a way. It would be a kind of legacy, a way to be remembered even after you're gone."

She crossed her arms over her chest, one finger tapping the top of one arm, her brow furrowed as she considered my suggestion. "You know, I kind of like that idea. If you're that interested, then sure, but on one condition."

She looked at me mischievously as if she'd heard me thinking about her and her deals. "I'll tell you my story, if you share yours as well. Tit for tat, we'll talk about me some tonight, in the morning you tell me some about you. How's that?"

I had no doubt that part of telling her mine would involve her coming back to her question of what I'd wanted as a reporter. She'd probably also want to know why I was there. I didn't want to tell her, not about that, not about them. But I was certain if I refused, she'd shut down on me, refuse to tell me more about herself. As selfish as I was, I couldn't bring myself to put my mediocre privacy above trying to save her life. Particularly knowing if she left and searched for information about me, she'd find out most of the story anyway. So with grim determination, I retrieved my notebook and pen from my bag.

"Sounds fair to me."

Even though it was her idea, for a moment she looked almost hesitant. But then she squared her shoulders as if mentally bracing herself. "Where should I begin?"

"Anywhere is fine. You can go chronologically or, if it's easier, in whatever order things come to you, I can always put it in order later."

"Okay." Her heavy sigh lingered in the tight space between us. It was the first gesture she'd made at that point of being anything other than happy-go-lucky, well other than the wanting to die thing. "I guess I'll start with Akihito and Noritaka then."

Akihito & Noritaka

THE GIRL WHO WOULD eventually become Yuna started life as a normal enough little girl. She was as cute and easy to care for a baby as any family could hope for. Alas, for her, she was the second child to be born to her middle-class parents. Her mother, Hiromi, was a hospital nurse. Her father, Takashi, was your average salaryman at an unremarkable company, paid decently enough, but would never be much more than he was then.

Neither of them had desired any more children, for in their minds they had already achieved perfection in their first child, their son Akihito. He had been born five years before Yuna's unplanned arrival, and for reasons we may never know, her parents seemed to have no room left in their hearts to love a second child even half so much.

From her very first day home of life, Yuna would be second to her brother in all things as far as her parents were concerned. It wasn't that they failed to care for her, unless one counts the hideous lack of love, or abused her beyond failing to build her up and dote on her, as any normal parents would. Instead, their preference was purely for Akihito, who they had already placed on such an unrealistic pedestal that there was no force on Earth that could topple it.

In their eyes, Akihito could do no wrong, while Yuna existed as a foil for her brother's awesomeness. So great was their parents' devotion to this singular cause that it made them distort reality to match their vision. Akihito was the smartest child, despite Yuna's grades consistently being higher. He was incredibly creative, in some unknown craft, while just a little encouragement and support for Yuna might have put her on the path of being a solid pianist. He was a born leader, while Yuna was the one who would have been the regular class representative had she been allowed.

But Akihito was blessed with the lethal combination of good looks, personality, and that rare sort of charm that enabled him to get out of any trouble with just a smile and a little cajoling. His pedestal extended far beyond his parents' support, though they were the worst of it. The other relatives in their family, his teachers at school, and later his employer; it didn't seem to matter, he was coated in a Teflon shield that resulted in no one viewing him as being able to do wrong. He was the sweet, devoted son, a loving brother, a charming, if spoiled child who would eventually grow into a dangerously charismatic young man.

And yet, for all that and their parents' blatant favoritism, the siblings held no hard feelings towards one another. Yuna was just as devoted to him as the rest, and in some ways, her pedestal was even higher than the one her parents had him on, though perhaps not entirely of her own volition. Akihito loved his newly arrived sister, doting on her in a way that her parents never could be bothered to. Just as he was the center of his parents' world, she soon enough became the center of his.

Sure, their early childhood was much like that of any siblings with a five-year age gap. They had fights and the sorts of "crises" that were life and death issues in one minute, forgotten the next as they ran off to play again. Normally, in such a family, one would expect Akihito to shift from playmate to vaguely disinterested older brother who grew tired of having a little girl always tagging along with him, but he did not. Rather, he gladly soaked up every drop of love she poured on him and took her with him almost everywhere. If he'd been allowed, he might very well have even taken her to class with him.

And pity the fool who dared treat her wrong or make her cry. Akihito's form of justice was swift, and often disturbingly violent, as those who loved him all too frequently turned a blind eye to his terrifying temper. Fortunately, their neighborhood was small enough that word spread quickly, and even the most stalwart of would-be-bullies gave Yuna a wide birth. It left her with few friends as well, for even those with good intentions feared her brother.

In some ways, the mental calisthenics their parents went through to keep Akihito positioned as an absolute angel were impressive. When he ambushed one foolish elementary school bully who stole Yuna's lunch, and proceeded to throw the boy into a nearby river and almost drowned him, he wasn't viewed as dangerous or evil. Instead, he was praised for being such a sweet and devoted brother, and his ministrations seen as "adorable".

Sadly, like most people, few bothered to look beneath the surface or stop to question those less than admirable qualities of his. Such as his disturbing possessiveness of Yuna, so deep that he was glad no one was willing to be her friend and he would quickly chase off anyone who had gotten up the nerve to try. He lavished her with love and praise, but cruelly shunned her if she dared give anyone else attention. Even with their parents, he tolerated her inexplicable love of them only reluctantly. Multiple times a day he demanded to know how much she loved him and only him.

Like many such violent, powerful youths, Akihito had a regular group of followers that only stopped short of being a gang by his being so socially acceptable. Any members who dared complain or express reservations about Yuna's near constant presence, or to look askance at how affectionate Akihito was towards her, was lucky to get away with just being exiled. Some found themselves violently removed from the gang. It was only a miracle that kept any of them from dying at his hands.

Akihito began serial dating at the age of fourteen. Within a few weeks of being with his first girlfriend, he pressured the girl into having sex. But she quickly tired of the little sister tagging along, much less sitting in the other room while they were wrestling around on the bed. The second one lasted even less time than the first. A year after he started dating, Akihito met seventeen-year-old Kira. Unlike the other girls, Kira had no issues with Yuna hanging around. She was even friendly to the little girl, at least as much as the jealous Akihito would tolerate, and would bring her treats. Her only demand was that Yuna not be quite so nearby when Akihito wanted to do all the deliciously naughty things he whispered in her ear about. Kira was a smart girl, and one of the few capable of handling Akihito beyond just fawning over him.

So it was that Akihito, for the lure of his hot older girlfriend's body, consented to leave Yuna in the trusted care of his best friend, Noritaka, during their sexual escapades. Friends since first grade, Noritaka was like family, not only to Akihito, but to Yuna and her parents as well. The trio was met with both families by much awwing and cooing when they were young and repeated exclamations of what fine boys both were for their tender care over Yuna. As far as they were concerned, Yuna's future was already secured, for the families had informally agreed that when they were old enough, Yuna would marry Noritaka, making the family bonds reality.

Alas, to Yuna's detriment, both sets of parents were idealistic, blind morons.

WHILE AKIHITO HAD LITTLE fear of his parent's recriminations if they caught him with a girl at home, Kira was less inclined to take the risk, particularly considering she was two years older than him. While her family was not so enamored with her as Akihito's, she could still remember her father's reaction the first, and only, time he caught her messing around at home. It wasn't the anger that had torn her up, it was the sheer disappointment. Even to this day, she struggled to mend the once close bond they shared. Though she'd toned down her friskiness since, something about Akihito had drawn her in enough that she'd relented to his flirting.

Fortunately, Akihito was prepared for such things and had already scoped out a nice private spot in a heavily wooded, mildly neglected, and barely used park. Whenever they were in the mood, the foursome would go there, with Yuna left in Noritaka's care in a clearing. Not yet ready to have Yuna knowing about sex and the like, Akihito always told her that he and Kira were just having a private talk, couple time like their parents liked to have, and that he'd be back soon.

The first few visits were innocent enough. Noritaka would entertain Yuna with his handheld game system or she'd read while he'd do homework. Akihito and Kira would return an hour or two later, and they would head out. Sometimes they'd stop for ice cream or to eat out, which always made Yuna happy as her family rarely went out for meals together. And once they were walking home alone together, Akihito would hold her hand and tell her stories and how much he loved her, and it was great fun all around.

Then one day, about fifteen minutes after Akihito had left them alone, Noritaka closed his school book and looked at ten-and-a-half-year-old Yuna where she sat working on her own classwork. Her dark hair was long, straight, and silky. It looked soft to the touch. Her wide amber eyes were often crinkled due to how much she smiled. Despite her parents, she was a cheerful girl. A sweet little girl who was growing up. He noticed how the first signs of breasts were pushing her shirt out a bit. If anyone had been willing to risk Akihito's wrath, she'd probably be getting teased unmercifully at school, but as gender was not an equalizer in who Akihito would assault, even the girls left her alone.

But Noritaka had noticed them, and how pretty his little pseudo-fiancée was growing up to be. "Hey, Yuna, come here a sec." With a smile, Yuna dutifully complied. "Do you know what Aki is back there doing with Kira right now?"

"Talking privately. About love and mushy stuff, I guess."

He chuckled, then reached out to play with her hand. "That's the polite way of putting it, I suppose. Actually they are back there having sex. It's what couples do. Your mom and dad to it too."

"Really?" Yuna looked at him curiously. She'd had sex education some, so she had a vague idea of what sex was, but she wasn't sure why Akihito would be doing it with Kira.

"Of course." He tugged her hand lightly until she was sitting in his lap, looking at him in such a trusting fashion that one would hope he felt some smidgen of guilt for what he was doing. Any sane or sensible person who'd born witness to Noritaka's expression as he looked at Yuna would have yanked her away from him and hidden her forever from his sight. But there were no such people around, and the adults in their lives were, as noted, disinclined to notice. He stroked her arm in a deliberately care-less fashion, as if unaware he was even doing it. "You know we'll get married one day, which makes us a couple already. But I bet you have never even been kissed before."

"Sure, my mom and dad kiss me all the time, and Nii-san too."

He laughed at her response. "Those are just family kisses. I mean a real kiss, the way a man kisses a woman, his woman?"

She furrowed her brow a moment as she tried to figure out the difference, then slowly shook her head. He smiled again, his hand now stroking her face while the other held her around the waist.

"You know I love you right? You're my girl, my wife-to-be, and I really want to kiss you like that. But I don't want to scare you, so I wanted to ask you first…can I?"

Yuna was still confused over the difference, but he hadn't told her anything she didn't already know. Her parents had repeatedly told her how glad they would be when she was old enough to marry Noritaka. They'd even said they'd sign so they could do it early instead of having to wait until she was twenty. As what he said all sounded right and normal, she nodded her consent.

Noritaka rubbed her cheek, her lips, then kissed her cheeks before tilting her head towards him. A moment later he pulled her a little closer and brushed his lips across hers. Between two adults, or even between himself and a girl his own age, it would have been a sweet, chaste first kiss. For Noritaka and Yuna, it was the first step in her ruination and his descent into unredeemable villainy.

When she didn't object, he kissed her again, and again.

Closed mouth kisses, light pecks and brushes, while eventually encouraging her to do the same. The whole while his hands rested on her bare legs, just below the edge of her skirt. Sometimes Yuna could feel his fingers playing with the fabric before his hand would jerk back. The monster in him hadn't fully awakened... yet.

Instead, he held himself back, limiting himself to kisses, over the clothes touches. But his sick desires could not be held at bay long by such banality, and soon he was "teaching" Yuna about open mouthed kissing, and touching her more intimately above her clothes. For her part, Yuna had no idea at the time that he was acting repugnant. She only knew what he'd told her, that it was "proper" for them to do as a couple. And that nothing he was doing necessarily hurt or felt unpleasant, so she could see no reason to doubt him.

An apologist might point out that Noritaka always limited that first year of contact to just kissing and that he never touched her under her clothes. And yes, it was some sliver of decency in him that seemed to keep him from going further, at least initially. One could also argue that he was just a child, innocently acting like a child and ignorant of his behaviors seeming predatory. It was true, he was still a child at fifteen, but said child had also blackmailed multiple girls into giving him sexually explicit pictures that he'd then shared with his friends. Said pictures would also be shown to Yuna further down the line. It was also rumored that the same "child" had joined Akihito in raping one of the latter's girlfriends for refusing to have sex with him. Noritaka joining in was considered appropriate punishment by both boys.

As she grew older, Yuna might have had a chance to

realize that Noritaka's actions with her were wrong and should be reported, but by that time, it was too late. She had no friends to give her console, no close relationships with teachers to talk to, and Noritaka had slyly planted in her mind that if she told, it would make her brother hate her and he'd force Noritaka to abandon her. Her parents were as useless; all she had to rely on was her abuser and her brother.

If this were a fairy tale story, Yuna would have confessed Noritaka's actions to Akihito and he would have acted as her knight, rescuing her from her abuser before it got any worse. But it is not and so any doubts that came up, Yuna would push aside because in her mind Noritaka would never, ever do anything to hurt her – this, at least, she was naively certain of.

By the time Yuna was twelve, Noritaka had started touching her under her clothes, stroking her chest, her stomach. By some sense of control, he managed to avoid completely defiling her body, but he would sit her on his lap and have her straddle the erection in his pants.

And always, always he told her of his love for her, how special and precious she was too him. Like any young girl, especially one so isolated as she, she drank it in and believed every single word. He and Akihito were the center of her world, and as much as her parents put her brother on a pedestal, she had the duo on one even higher. It was an honor and a level of devotion that neither deserved.

Present

WHEN YUNA STOPPED SPEAKING at length, I looked up from my pages of notes to check on her while trying to remember if I had any tissues in my bag, certain she would be crying at this point. But she wasn't. If anything, I'd have said her expression was a wistful one, as if she'd been recounting a far more pleasant childhood than the one she had just related to me.

She glanced at me, then laughed lightly. "I know, I know, I should be horribly upset. I should be cursing his name with my every breath and ranting and raving about how his molestation damaged me. But, I really can't bring myself to hate him." She paused, as if waiting to gauge my reaction. "I suppose one might say I was in denial, or just screwed up, but at the time, it didn't hurt me, not physically. To me, he was Noritaka, sweet kind Noritaka. My brother's best friend, the man I'd already been told repeatedly I'd marry one day. Any time something he did scared me or made me even look upset, he'd stop."

"So, even though you know it was wrong now, you still aren't angry at him?"

"Hmm…" She laid down on her side, her hands tucked under her face as she looked at me. "No, not really. The memories of those days are not painful ones for me. There was no great trauma, no physical or verbal attacks to make the rest negative. I did eventually get angry at him about something else, but I'll tell you about that another time."

Before I could ask another follow up question, she gave a pointed, and somewhat exaggerated yawn, clearly signaling the end of today's interview. Glancing at my watch as I put away my notes, I realized she'd talked for nearly three hours. Still, part of me wanted to keep working a bit, but I suspected if I suggested doing so while she slept, that would be a rule violation. Besides, the long walk and the lateness of the hour had my own body giving hints that it wouldn't mind sleeping as well.

We headed outside for a final bathroom break a bit away from our clearing, using our flashlights to light the way. She kept me in sight, again, but was at least kind enough to not point her flashlight at anything untoward. As we returned to the tent, she pulled her hair out of its ponytail and switched it to a braid.

Her tent was a lightweight model, no doubt in consideration of her size and needing to carry it alone. Though it was a nice size, at least big enough for us to sit inside with relative comfort, once we were both lying side by side on her open sleeping bag, the space felt minuscule. We'd already put our backpacks into the little covered bit to the side, so there wasn't any way to add room. I squished myself as far from her as I could, near the wall of the tent. The last thing I wanted was to be another man who took advantage of her.

The quiet stretched on in the darkness of the space. I debated trying to sneak out and find help, but in the dark, there was no way I'd be able to find my way out, much less make it back before she would wake up and notice I was gone. She also slept on the side with the alcove, which meant reaching over her to grab the flashlight. I wondered if tomorrow I could somehow trick her into letting me go in her bag to find those sleeping pills. If I slipped her just two or three, it would knock her out long enough to get help for her but not endanger her.

"Adachi?" I jumped at the sound of her voice, feeling guilty for the track my thoughts had taken. I thought she'd already fallen asleep. I cleared my throat before answering her with a simple yes. "Why are you way over there? You'll be cold… You can't have very much blanket on you."

I wanted to deny it, but a shiver betrayed me. It was getting cooler, even with the closed tent trapping our body heat snugly inside. Of course, if she was that concerned about my welfare, she could have left with me when it was still nice and warm instead of having us stuck out in a place where it would likely drop as low as 4° Celsius overnight. Still, being snarky wouldn't help me convince her otherwise, so I vaguely shrugged. "I'll be okay. I wouldn't want to make you uncomfortable."

I thought I heard her giggle before I felt her small hand

tugging my shirt. "Then come over here where it's warmer. You're making me feel like you think I'm a leper or something."

This time, I didn't try to hide the heavy sigh that escaped me, but still I complied, shifting to lie near her in the middle of the tent. "Better?"

"Much!" She wrapped her arms around me, snuggling up against me in a way that made me think briefly of Hiyori. When we had been happy, we'd regularly fallen asleep in a similar fashion. But Hiyori was my girlfriend, at the time anyway, and Yuna was a girl wanting to die.

"Um, Yuna?" I tried to keep my tone relatively neutral, even as my mind was going nuts trying to figure out what she was doing. It was chilly, sure, but it wasn't cold enough yet to need to be that close.

"You don't like this?" she asked even as she shifted in a way that suggested she knew part of me did. She was so damn warm, and it felt nice to have someone lying beside me again. A certain fourteen centimeters of myself really liked it, a part of myself I thought had died with the Nakamuras.

After shifting slightly to avoid her detecting my erection, I grunted noncommittally. In this game, she made all the rules anyway. "I guess it's okay. I mean it is going to be colder later so if you think it's necessary."

Her giggle was unmistakable this time as she gave me a squeeze. "Good night, Adachi. I look forward to learning more about you in the morning."

The Second Day

Present

I'D LIKE TO THINK having someone as cute and warm as
Yuna wrapped so close against me would act as a shield for
the usual dreams, but alas, it didn't. If anything, being
here in the forest only made them worse. Now instead of
just seeing the Nakamura's standing their asking why,
they'd become more translucent and terrifying. Their
ghostly visions chased me down an endless corridor, demanding to know why I killed them and asking when they
would get their justice. The me in my dreams shouted
pointless apologies and swore justice was coming soon;
there was just a little more work to be done first.

When their images weren't haunting me, I found myself dreaming of Hiyori. It was the first time I'd seen her
in my dreams since the first few weeks after our breakup.

I wish it had been a pleasant dream of our happier times, but the Hiyori in my dreams called me a sell-out, a coward, a liar, and a murderer as she marched around me with others carrying signs that again mentioned justice for the Nakamuras. Sadly, much of that dream had been more realistic, other than her being part of some rally against me.

Suffice to say, it was a long night that brought little in the way of true rest. When I gave up attempting to sleep, I found Yuna still nestled snug against my body, her arms around me and, to my horror, mine around her. I tried to release her without waking her, but I soon realized she was watching my amateur acrobatics with a bemused expression.

"Morning!" she said brightly, before taking mercy on me and letting me go to sit up into a stretch.

"Morning…" I yawned as I sat up. My body ached all over. It had been too long since I'd done any sort of camping, much less bare bones. While her sleeping bag wasn't the worse kind, it hadn't given my spoiled muscles and joints nearly enough cushioning from the hard ground.

"Um, Yuna…I know you just woke up, but I kind of need to go to the bathroom."

"Well of course you do. Don't most people in the morning? Come on." She led the way out of the tent, stretching again before moving a couple of meters from the campsite. It was still early enough that we had to use my flashlight to see where we were stepping. As with the day before, we took turns. While I went, she leaned against a tree not far enough away, watching me as usual. When she saw me look at her, she even gave me a little wave.

I swear it was as if she had no concept of personal

boundaries. She'd dropped the honorific from my name almost immediately, without any sign she thought of asking if it was okay first. I'd also quickly noticed she was very touchy-feely, regularly touching my arms while walking or my legs when we were in the tent.

Nothing in her story so far hinted at that being her normal nature, though maybe it was some twisted way of taking back control after having gone through such events due to having none? While I'd let her get away with saying she was unaffected by the molestation, I hadn't believed her. There just didn't seem to be anyway someone could go through that and not have it change them in some manner.

While I was certainly no psychologist, I'd taken the intro course at university. I'd also enjoyed several conversations with my friend Shinji's wife about her experiences with going to therapy and her course work to become a real therapist herself. What would she make of Yuna, hmm? A broken woman hiding behind an overly cheerful smile? Someone whose subconscious was causing her to exert control in the oddest of ways just to take back the control she lost? Presumably suffering from depression despite what she'd said, else she'd have no desire to die. Of course, my arm-chair analysis was worth about what anyone would have paid for it.

For now, my biggest tasks were to get her to change her mind about dying, and the sooner the better so I could get her on her way and I could finish what I came to do. And to get her to trust me enough to stop watching me go to the bathroom before I had to do more than urinate, which was already hard enough to do with an audience.

Once we returned to the tent, breakfast was a combination of the sandwich I brought and an apple she had, each split evenly. Sitting there in the lantern light, it again struck me how normal it seemed, and that if things had been different, it might have been nice getting to know her.

"Hmmm, it will be at least an hour before we can pack up and move on," she remarked after glancing at her wrist watch. "Hey, how much money do you have on you?"

"Um, not sure… I guess I could check." I didn't try to hide the questioning in my tone, but she just watched expectantly as I pulled out my wallet and counted. I debated lying about the amount, but she'd shown herself to be too perceptive to fall for it easily, and it would not have helped my goal of getting privacy for bathroom duties. "About 20,000 yen or so. Why?"

"Just wondering. Was contemplating something we might do later in the week. I have 40,000 myself, so we should have plenty."

"For what?" The place wasn't exactly teeming with stores unless she intended to go back to the entrance. But I doubt she would risk that, it would be easy enough for me to get help then. I wasn't surprised when her answer to my question was just another enigmatic smile. She was far better at keeping her secrets than I, I supposed. With a mild shrug, I returned my wallet to my pocket.

"With that out of the way… now it's your turn."

I stumbled on the sudden change in topic. "My turn?"

This time she laughed. "For sharing your story." With a pause, she tapped a slender finger against her cheek a few times. "Let's see…how about you tell me how and why you became a reporter, and what your dream was seems like a fair exchange for what I've told you so far."

I wished she'd just asked for a more quid pro quo exchange. Telling of my dull childhood as the middle son of a perfectly ordinary, boring family would have been an easy enough task, if a bit snooze inducing. I suppose it was still better than having to tell her why I'd stopped being a reporter, though I was sure that would only be a temporary reprieve. She was just giving me a warm up morning, I was sure of it.

She cleared her throat in a pointed reminder that she was waiting. Pushing aside my concerns over what would be coming during our next interview session, I turned my memory back to my teenage years when the reporting bug had first hit me.

"I guess it started in high school. When I was a first year, I wasn't interested in any of the sports clubs, as I'm not particularly athletic. In middle school, my teacher had encouraged me to consider writing, as she thought I was decent at it, so on a whim I joined the journalism club. Our main duties consisted of putting out a weekly school newspaper."

"Oh, I've heard some schools have those. What kind of stuff did yours have in it?"

"The usual stuff I guess, upcoming events, reporting on the results of sports and stuff, feature profiles on people, things like that. We also did articles each week on different club activities and stuff to help highlight them, give them a bit of publicity. In a lot of ways, we mimicked our town's local paper, though without sections like business or crime. Oh, and the manga club contributed weekly comic strips for us too."

"Cool! So what did you write?"

"I did the profile articles about the top students, teachers, and administrators." I shrugged. "They were mostly fluff pieces since we weren't trying to reveal any dark secrets or embarrass them, it was just a nice way for other students to get to know the key people in school and the best students."

She made a scoffing sound. "You never wrote about regular students?"

"No, I guess not. It wasn't that they weren't important or anything, just less interesting, I guess."

"How do you know if you never talked to them?"

I couldn't think of a good answer. The truth was, I'd wondered the same thing back then and had even proposed expanding our interviews to the whole student body, versus just the top scorers on tests and top athletes. The idea had been laughed at by the rest of the club and dismissed as a joke. Lacking the confidence to push the idea, I'd laughed it off too and let them think just that: a joke, a poor attempt to lighten things up during an otherwise dull meeting.

"Is that what made you decide to be a reporter?" she asked, seeming to accept my silence as my answer.

"Yeah. At first it was just something to do because I thought I had to be in a club, but I found I enjoyed the interviewing and talking to people. I don't know that my writing was the best, but people seemed to like my stories. But it was my adviser who first prompted me to look at it as a potential career. By my 3rd year, I'd decided that it was exactly what I wanted to do, so I applied to Waseda University and majored in journalism. As soon as I graduated, I applied for a few places and got hired at my current job."

Though Yuna smiled at me, it felt a little sad. "You said before that you did lifestyle reporting when you started and now you do business stuff. But what do you really want to write about? What was your dream when you left college?"

I'd hoped she'd forgotten about that part of her question since it had brightened enough outside to let us leave. I should have known she wouldn't let me get away without answering. Part of me wanted to refuse, to push her boundaries a bit, to see how she would respond. But I couldn't bring myself to do it. There was the fear that she'd end our deal, of course, but it also seemed grossly unfair. What she was asking of me paled in comparison to what she'd told me so far. How could I refuse while asking her to continue, even letting me take notes as she went? It violated the normal way reporting and interviewing went, but I'd already come to terms that this was the way it needed to be with us.

"While at school for my degree, I was exposed to the various areas of focus reporters have. Some of our assignments had us reporting stories specifically through those lenses, which really gave you a feel for the differences between how a business reporter and a regular news reporter would talk about the same story. From those experiences, I quickly realized my passion lay in being an investigative reporter. I wanted to dig down through important events and find the real story behind the story that's presented to the public. I thought by doing that I would be a hero in my own way, not strong or terribly brave, but bringing the truth to the people. I thought it was the most important type of work one could do as a journalist." I paused to take a deep breath. "Do you know what the Pulitzer Prize is?"

"It's a big award for journalists, right, like the best award you can get?"

"Pretty much. It actually covers a variety of writing pursuits, even books and music, but for me, it was all about the journalism prizes. I don't think most people realize they have over a dozen categories just in the journalism area alone! There are prizes for breaking news, investigative reporting, local, national, and so forth. It's an American prize, but I thought the people who won had to be the best of the best. So I read every story that had won in that category, as well as several of the close contenders. I studied the writers' careers and read any interview I could find. People like Bill Dedman, who exposed racial prejudices in mortgage lending in certain areas, and Brian Deer, who debunked that horrible research that claimed autism was caused by vaccines that led to the anti-vaccination movement and allowed previously beaten diseases to return."

"What went wrong?"

I started, though by now I should have been used to her keen ability to hone in on my most vulnerable areas. It wasn't something I wanted to admit, to say out loud, but she was watching me with that look of expectation tinged with pity. Did she already know?

"I realized people don't want the truth. Many of the people we call investigative journalists here, they don't investigate, they don't dig deep. They accept whatever is told to them by the government, by the big companies. If you try to report the truth, you find yourself being sued, maybe even jailed. There are rumors some reporters have even disappeared if they try. The press here has limits, and it feels as if the truth is allowed only when it doesn't affect the big players. Tear apart the little people, that's all well and good, but not the important ones, not the ones with power and money who most need to be watched. I realized my dream was a fantasy, one that could never be in today's Japan."

Yuna took my hand between hers, stroking my palm with her thumb. She didn't try to tell me I was wrong or even that I could change things; she just quietly nodded, as if she understood all too well how pointless it was.

A few minutes later, she suggested we get moving. We packed up the camping supplies then after making sure we'd cleaned up behind ourselves, we headed back out into the woods. I offered to carry her bag for her, but she declined. Much like the day before, we trudged along through the woods, seemingly at random. Around midday, we stopped to take a rest break.

We meandered around, at some point crossing from the east side to the west, though I only realized this because we crossed over the main path that I'd walked in on. I think it was the same path anyway, as I was pretty sure there was only one except for the break off to the caves that was near the entrance.

Whenever we passed a stream, we'd stop to refill our respective water bottles, even if they were only partially empty. It was Yuna's idea, but I understood it. It was always better to have it and not need it than the other way around. Though I suspected that as heavy as the air was, we could have sucked on some moss, if needed, to get some water.

If we came across any guide lines, we carefully ducked under or over them, as appropriate. Yuna showed just as little interest as me in following them right then. It perhaps made me a bit cold, but I already had one life to save,

I couldn't handle another, or worse getting there too late.

Our walk that day was a mix of quiet companionship and simple, mundane conversation. As if in mutual agreement that we needed a break from heavier topics, we stuck to simpler conversations, like favorite foods, restaurants, TV shows, music, and the like. When we discovered we were both a fan of pop star Psy, we shared a few minutes singing off-tune to some of his songs.

It was an oddly cheerful way to spend the day in such a gloom-filled place. I suppose it also seemed odd since, in many ways, I'd become her voluntary hostage in that place. And yet, despite my mild irritation at being "stuck" with her, I didn't mind spending time with her. She was a cheerful girl and when we talked, I enjoyed the conversations. It was odd having someone else in control of my fate, to a degree, but in some ways, it was also a relief. The last few weeks, I'd struggled to even decide on what to eat, and now I just followed her steps as we walked around, wrote the story she told me to, and answered the questions she asked. In my becoming a hostage, I found a strange sense of freedom from the burden of living.

Still, as the light began waning, a blend of dread and anticipation filled me. I knew once we stopped and made camp, we'd continue with her story. I didn't want to know the rest, but at the same time, I had to. I had to know if that was why she was here now, or was it some other reason? The part of me that loved investigation, that had foolishly dreamed of being a truth teller, had latched on to her tale. I would not be satisfied until I knew how it ended.

That night, once we were settled in another clearing and in the tent, Yuna pulled two pouches out of her backpack. "Retorts okay for dinner tonight?"

"What are those?"

"Basically pre-made meals that we can heat by boiling them in some water." She pulled a small pot from her backpack. "They are kind of like the MREs the army uses, though tastier. We can grab some water from the stream, then it will just take a bit to heat using these Sterno cans."

"Oh, okay, sure, that sounds fine." The more I realized she'd come prepared to stay awhile, the more I felt certain she would leave with me at the end of the week. That maybe all she really needed was what I was giving her now, the chance to tell her story, to let someone else know of her pain and sorrows.

"Good. Meat and potato stew, chicken stew, or oden?"

"Meat please, if that's okay."

After we finished eating, I retrieved my notebook and pen. "Well, shall we continue?"

She nodded, with perhaps the saddest expression she'd ever given me.

Brother No More

For Yuna, childhood was not a time of innocent play and increasing studies, but secrets. Horrible, life-altering secrets. Noritaka was only one part of the issue, and while he certainly was vile, he kept his activities only to the visits to the woods. And he, at least, had some lines he never crossed. Nor did he try to control her as some form of property; in his twisted mind, they were just kick-starting their eventual marriage.

But for Yuna there was a far worse secret than Noritaka, that of her brother Akihito. Everyone knew he was a devoted brother, perhaps overly protective and maybe too inclined to see her as his and his alone, but the family didn't mind, Yuna was too young and too molded to complain, and anyone else feared his wrath too much. Even

Noritaka had long given up trying to get Akihito to at least allow his sister to have some friends her own age.

But, the thing no one knew was how he'd insist they take their baths together when they were home alone, even though she was far too old for it to still be a thing. Or how he'd wrap his arms around her in the tub and hold her tight against him, telling her how much he loved her. Nor did anyone know how he would encourage her to sleep with him, nestled in his arms like a lover. Or that he'd told her more than once that she would not be marrying Noritaka when she grew up, rather she'd marry him because he, Akihito, loved her more than anyone else ever could. To say such things was confusing for a young girl would be an understatement. In the end, her mind protected her as best it could by compartmentalizing the two. Noritaka was the person who loved her most in the woods, her brother at home, and that was that.

The secrets spread throughout her early life, from single digits until her early teen years. The main difference between her two molesters was in degree and pace of escalation. Akihito limited himself to his words, to hugging, chaste family kisses, and to the sleeping and baths. He earnestly believed he was in love with his little sister, and he was determined he would not defile her pure love for him by touching her sexually until she was old enough and ready to love him back the same way. Though as she grew older, and her feminine curves began forming, he found even that twisted morality beginning to weaken.

The problem with secrets was that they could only truly remain a secret if you were the only one who knew them. It happened one Friday evening while their parents were away for the weekend visiting relatives. Akihito and Yuna had been left home to study for exams, Yuna for her middle school entrance exams, and Akihito for his college ones.

That night, Akihito had been especially attentive with Yuna, touching her arms and waist a lot. When they made dinner, he stayed close to her, crowding into her personal space and pressing himself against her. Later, as they sat in the living room, he pulled her onto his lap. "Yuna, you love me the most, right?"

"Of course, Nii-san. You are my favorite person in the world." She'd said it innocently, smiling as she hugged him. Long used to his demanding regular confirmations of love, she knew this routine well. What was different this time was when he'd cupped her face with his hand and pulled her towards him, brushing his lips against hers for a moment before looking back to see her reaction.

Most girls might have been horrified or confused, but for Yuna, it was no different from what Noritaka had done. All the years of his grooming made her certain that Nii-san now loved her even more, so she just smiled back at him when he pulled away.

He kissed her again, sliding his tongue into her mouth. By now Yuna knew enough to kiss him in return. Her returning his affection, his kissing her, it was the stuff of his every fantasy. He should have been thrilled to finally give in to his craven desires and it play out just as it had in his dreams, but instead he was left shaken and confused. When they broke apart, their breathing ragged, he gave her an undefinable look. "Yuna, have you ever been kissed like that before?"

She hesitated a moment. Noritaka had told her not to tell anyone, but at the same time, lying to Akihito would leave him furious with him. Of the two, she feared losing her brother's love more than having to deal with Noritaka's annoyance. Besides, it wasn't as if they had done anything wrong and surely, he'd already told her brother? They told each other everything. So maybe Akihito was testing Yuna's loyalty and honesty. He did that sometimes, asking her questions to see if she'd tell the truth.

"Noritaka of course."

But instead of smiling and looking happy with her for staying honest, his face darkened with anger and Akihito grabbed her arms in a bruising grip. "Noritaka? He, he's been kissing you like that?"

Shaking a little, she nodded again.

"When he was kissing you, did he do anything else to you? Like touch you and stuff?"

The coldness in his voice had her more terrified than anything, so she quickly told him everything she and Noritaka had done in the woods while he'd been with Kira. By the time she was done, the look on Akihito's face had her wanting to run away, but he was still holding her arms, the places his finger held her now white from the pressure.

"That son of a bitch. When I…" He looked at her and, as if realizing he was scaring her, finally released her arms and pulled her into his embrace. "Did he hurt you?"

"No, never. He wouldn't hurt me, you know that. He's part of our family."

"Yeah, family…"

"Aki, are you angry at me? Did I do something wrong?"

"No, it isn't you. I promise." He smiled at her now, then caressed her cheek before kissing her face. In a romantic movie, it would have been the start of a beautiful love making scene. In the living room of their house, it was the start of her final downfall. "Come here, baby. Will you show me what he's done to you, what he taught you to do? I bet it would feel really good."

The last of his restraints dropped, Akihito took his sister much as he had his past girlfriends, the many substitutes over the years he'd used to relieve himself with while holding his desire for his sister in check. His arms wrapped around her and stroked her back before diving under her shirt to touch her breasts while encouraging her to touch him, to explore his body with her hands.

Even at that age, Yuna had no idea that she was "supposed" to be enjoying the physical aspects of it herself; she went along with things to make him happy and to erase his anger. While she couldn't fully understand the idea of desire yet, she did know there was *something* there, something she'd begun to notice when Noritaka touched her as well. Strange feelings in her body, sensations that she wasn't sure if she liked or didn't. Remember, she was yet unknowing that what they did was wrong, so for her it was purely a matter of how it felt. And her brother's strokes as he lay her down on the floor, soft and reverent against her body now, felt pleasant. The way he kissed her made her tingly in a weird, but not necessarily bad, way.

He pulled off her shirt so he could kiss and suck on her breasts. Noritaka had done it too, though he'd never taken her shirt off because he didn't want to risk getting caught with her needing to dress. Nor had it felt quite the way it felt with Akihito now, though if you'd asked her why she wouldn't have been able to explain it. It might have been purely different in the levels of love, for while she did love Noritaka, she truly did love Akihito more, for he'd made sure it was so from the day she was born. And while Nor-itaka desired her, Akihito, in his dark twisted mind, loved her to a level that none could hope to meet, nor would any sane person want to try.

There was also the great difference in the mannerisms of their abuse, for Noritaka had always been nervous, with it always at the forefront of his mind that Akihito could return at any moment, with little warning other than the crunching of leaves. While now, Akihito loved her with-out fear, without worries, for he knew they were alone and would be until Sunday. She was his, his at last.

"Yuna," his voice had a strange tightness to it as he said her name after kissing her lips. "Did Noritaka ever make you feel good or did he just make himself feel good?"

"What do you mean?"

"Do you know what it means to cum?"

"Oh, what he does sometimes?"

"Yeah, did he make you cum?"

She shook her head. As far as she knew that was some-thing men did when she did the things with her mouth on them that Noritaka liked.

"Now listen to me, okay? You're mine now, and mine alone. Noritaka won't be touching you again, understand? Only I get to do this to you, to love you like this. It's spe-cial, it's only for me to do and he knew that. I'm sorry he abused your trust like that."

"Okay." She smiled uncertainly, worried he was angry again.

"Good girl." He smiled, though it was strained. "Now let me show you something special, okay? Relax baby, let me make you feel good."

He kissed his way back down her body, following the

path of his hand that was already pushing down the bottom of her pajamas. With them and her panties gone, he slid his fingers between her legs, rubbing her in ways Noritaka never had. At first it just felt interesting, not much different from other touching, but then she became aware of a warmth spreading through her, and a strange longing for something undefinable. Then her brother moved and kissed her there, shocking her still as his tongue touched her down there.

"Nii-san?" she squeaked out. Unsure what to make of it, she wiggled under his efforts. It seemed so weird.

"Shh, it's okay, baby, it's okay. Just relax, you'll like this, I promise." As he spoke in that soothing voice, he used his free hand to grab her hand and give it a squeeze, letting her keep hold of it as he continued. On and on it went, her unknowingly being driven to her first orgasm, innocently lying in thrall of the sensations welling up inside her. It felt as if someone had turned the heater on to full blast even though she knew the room was still at a comfortable temperature.

A twisting, tightening feeling had her wiggling some more, but now her brother just held her hips so that she couldn't escape while letting her thrash about. Suddenly she found herself screaming as a flood of physical pleasure rushed through her body. It was a feeling that she'd never known before or imagined was even possible. When it was done, she could only lay panting on the floor while Akihito moved so he lay on top of her, kissing her.

"See, that felt good, right?"

Her head was still fuzzy, making his voice seem muffled. Dazed and still confused as to what just happened, she nodded slowly.

"Good girl. Just remember, that's something only I can make you feel, okay? That's just for us to do." He shifted to lay beside her and snuggled against her, then moved her hand to wrap it around his jutting penis. "Stroke it for me, okay? Make me feel like that too."

Shaking off the left overs of the orgasm, she did as she was told, using her hands to stroke him, then at his encouragement her mouth, just as Noritaka had taught her. The sounds he made worried her at first until he assured her they meant he loved what she was doing. With his hands buried in her hair, he guided her efforts, until his grip tightened and then he grunted. Seconds later her mouth was filled with something hot, salty, and nasty. She gagged and coughed and she moved away from him and stared at him in confusion.

He quickly sat up and kissed her all over her face. "Sorry, baby, I figured he'd taught you how to swallow. It's okay, you did good, so good. You're my sweet, special girl. I love you so much."

While Akihito had her sleep in his bed that night, he didn't take their activities any further, contenting himself with holding her tight against him. To Yuna, everything seemed fine. Her brother loved her even more now and was so pleased with her. He'd even made her feel such a wild, thrilling way. Already she'd forgotten the flash of anger he'd displayed when he'd learned about her and Noritaka's woodland activities.

But Akihito hadn't forgotten. Saturday, they went to school the same as always, with him walking her to school before continuing to his high school. Next year, she'd be heading to high school, while he would go on to college, but he'd already decided to go to the one locally, so he could still walk her to school. That her parents saw nothing wrong with his reasoning was even more indication of how blind they were to their favored son's warped mind.

Before leaving her at the gate, Akihito told her not to wait for him that afternoon as he had an after school activity that would make him run late. Instead she was to go grocery shopping for dinner then go straight home and wait for him. Usually when he had to do that sort of thing, especially on the half day Saturdays, he was home by 3 at the latest. With him being a 3rd year, his activities were mostly curtailed in favor of preparing for the practice exams. But today, he didn't come home until 5, and when he did, his hands were all cut up.

"Nii-san!" She ran over to him as soon as she saw him, horrified at the sight of her brother's broken skin and the blood marring the white surface. "Are you okay?"

"I'm fine, baby girl, just fine. Had a little spill, that's all. Don't cry like that now, it doesn't even hurt anymore, I promise." He hugged her and kissed the top of her head. "I'm gonna wash up then we can make dinner, okay?"

"Okay…" she said with a sniffle. As she watched him walk away, she realized he wasn't wearing his school uniform anymore, but had changed at some point into some other outfit. Maybe she'd misunderstood his saying it was a school activity and instead he'd been with friends? He didn't usually wear his school clothes when he hung out with them as the schools tended to frown on students being seen around town in their uniforms if they weren't going to and from school.

When Akihito came back to where she waited in the living room, most of the blood was gone from his hands and bandages covered the worst looking of his wounds.

He swore again that he was just fine and shooed her into the kitchen to start cooking their meal. It wouldn't be too long before she would learn the source of his bruises.

After Akihito's hands had healed, he took her to the woods. Unlike all the other times, it was just the two of them. Akihito had broken up with his girlfriend the same weekend he'd let himself touch Yuna; she'd been the second since Kira had finally clued into his weirdness and dumped him a few months ago. Strangely, Noritaka did not join them either. When Yuna asked about him, Akihito had mumbled that he was busy and that this trip was just for them.

There in the woods, he gave in to the last of his desires, taking her in the clearing in the same spot he'd always seen her waiting with Noritaka. There, he was sweet, gentle, loving her as if she was a porcelain doll that he was afraid to break. Of course, his viewing of the encounter as "love making" didn't negate the depravity of what he did, or that he'd stolen the last bit of innocence from his thirteen-year-old sister, his full-blooded baby sister, who even then knew somewhere in the back of her mind that it was wrong. But he played her body with all the skills he'd built up over his years of sexual promiscuity, allowing him to make even her young, inexperienced body crave what he was offering and to push any niggling bits of doubt as she found herself again flooded with that tight heat that made her forget all reason for the briefest of moments.

It was a summer afternoon that thrust her from child to woman without any of the preparation she truly needed, leaving her mentally unprepared for the world she would soon find herself lost in. In his desperate act of twisted love, Akihito cursed his sister to a life that would have made him castrate himself had he been able to foresee it, but all he could see was that moment, that time when his jealousy and needs had him pushing her into the soft leaves to claim what he thought was rightfully his.

Present

WE SAT IN SILENCE awhile, giving me time to realize what had left me so bothered by her recounting of her brother's rape. Again, she'd never used that term for it. Nor had she referred to it as molestation or abuse. During the entire story, she'd clearly called it love making. As I realized Akihito had gone far further than Noritaka, I'd been expecting he was the target of her hate and rage, but no, she'd spoken of him like a missed and fondly remember lover. When she'd been a child, too ignorant to know it was wrong, I could understand, but now? Surely she knew better? I hesitated to ask, but I knew I had to if I wanted to get the full story.

"Yuna, I… you know what they did to you was wrong, right? Noritaka and Akihito?"

For the first time since we met, she seemed uncertain and hesitant to answer, as she sat there in the warm glow of the tent light, wringing her hands together in an almost unconscious motion. As I waited, she shifted position to rest her elbows on her legs and her mouth between the backs of her hands with her eyes downcast before releasing a small sigh. Finally, she looked up at me, looking so torn that for a moment I could see the young girl she'd been back then in her expression. "You told me you had longed for the truth. Do you still want it now, or would you rather the warm, pleasant lies people would expect to hear?"

Part of me screamed to say I wanted the lies, the comfort of knowing she'd responded "correctly", but that would make the whole exercise pointless, and go against what I'd told her. To ask for the lies would destroy the fragile trust we were building between us. "The truth, always please."

A small smile teased her lips, and she gave me a look of approval before continuing. "Logically, yes, I know it was wrong. I'm not an idiot or anything. Clinically, they both were child molesters, especially Noritaka starting when I was so young. But, as I said before, neither of them ever physically hurt me. The entire time, as far as I knew, I was loved and protected by the two most important people in my world, and the things we did made them happy and overall, they felt good to me too.

"I know from a neutral point of view, they manipulated me, used my love and theirs to get what they wanted. They taught me things that likely altered my thinking from what was 'normal' and screwed me up mentally in ways. But I can't really be neutral about it, since it was me living it. And in truth, I love them, I love them both. I did then, and I still do now. At least, the men I thought they were." Her last words were almost lost in her sleeve, but I caught the hint of sadness there. "And wrong as it is, I loved my brother as a man as much as my brother, though I do wonder how much of that love is truly real romantic love, versus just a warped version of our familial love?"

I had no way to answer her question, nor did she seem to expect one. Silence returned, briefly. I debated asking if she wanted to continue, but she now sat with her knees pulled against her chest, her arms wrapped around them. Nothing in her posture indicated any desire to talk more tonight. If anything, it seemed to be a cry to be held, to chase the pain away. But still, the reporter in me knew we had time for more. Before I could prompt her either way, though, she took the choice out of my hands as she so often did.

Uncurling from her position she moved over to me, sliding between my legs to wrap her arms around me. "Hold me for a while, Adachi. Make me nice and warm tonight."

I couldn't find it in me to argue with that slightly pleading voice, so I nodded. Soon enough we were lying in the sleeping bag in the center of the tent, Yuna snuggled against me like a cat, my arms around her at her request. I was tired, but my mind was too busy racing over everything we'd talked about so far. In hearing her story, I was horrified, of course, but I was already seeing the spread in the papers, a series of reports, along with side pieces on incidences of child abuse and resources in Japan. I doubted Yuna was the only victim, but was it a widespread issue not being discussed, or an isolated, but important one needing to be brought to light?

Suddenly my brain short circuited and every synapse that led to rational, intelligent thought began to rapidly shut down as I realized that Yuna's hand had shifted in such a way that she was stroking my crotch in an unmistakably deliberate fashion.

"Yuna." My voice sounded strangled even to my own ears.

"Hmmm?" Her reply sounded like a half purr as she rubbed her face against my chest.

"Um, your hand…what are you…?"

She laughed, a rich, earthy laugh that triggered a physical response in me without regard for my brains attempts at keeping control. "Adachi, surely you've had fun like this before?"

"Well, yes, I just…"

Her other arm wrapped around me and pulled me even closer against her.

"You seem to want me too… at least this does."

God help me, I knew she had to be all kinds of messed up. She'd come there to kill herself and the story of her life was going down an ever-darkening hole. And yet, my body responded to the feel of her hand and the way her lips brushed the underside of my scruffy jaw. I tried to think of some way to deflect her kindly, but then I made the mistake of looking down. Her lips touched mine, causing a hunger inside me that defeated me before I could even think to stop it.

I found myself returning her kiss, drinking in the taste of her like a man dying of thirst. How long had it been since I felt the softness of a woman in my arms? Surely that's all it was, I'd gone too long without sex, that's the only reason I could have for responding to her. But she was not the woman to reacquaint myself with such pleasures with, I knew this. I tried to regain control of myself.

"Yuna…we shouldn't…this is…"

"Why not? You're single. I'm single. We're here. It's cold. You feel nice." She punctuated each little sentence with a kiss. Every touch of her lips weakened my resolve that much more.

"But…" I tried again, but she just used the opportunity to kiss me more thoroughly, her tongue slipping into my mouth as she pressed her body against mine. Her breasts were small, but nice and round. My disobedient hands ran down her body, studying her curves along the way. She was slender, but not so thin that she felt starved.

I'd like to say I was a better man than this, that I fought off whatever desire had possessed me for this broken woman. I'd like to say that I was able to somehow turn her attentions aside without hurting her feelings and that we simply agreed to go to sleep. But I'd just be lying.

With a moan, I wrapped my arms around her and gave in to her demands. Near feverish with need, I kissed her mouth, her cheeks, her neck as my hand slid down and back up under her shirt to explore her breasts. Part of me kept expecting it to be a trap, that she would turn me away with a haughty laugh at any moment, or worse, that she would realize what she'd started and shrink from me in terror.

But no, if anything my response was all it took to get her even more ramped up. Her fingers dug into my hair as she encouraged me with her body. The groans and moans coming from her made it clear she was on as wild a high as I was. When I rolled her over onto her back and pushed her shirt over her head, she impatiently plucked at mine. As soon as it was gone, she dug her fingers into my skin, kneading my chest before wrapping her arms around me and letting her nails lightly rake my skin.

Somewhere in there, as I pulled off her pants, a moment of sanity returned. "Yuna, are you sure…"

"Yes, don't stop now. Hurry, Adachi, please!"

With that impassioned plea, the last of my rational brain left me to my own devices, and within moments I was plunging inside her. When I came, I paused only long enough to get hard again, taking the brief lull to bring her to orgasm with my fingers. I don't know how long we went at it before we finally collapsed with sheer exhaustion, the tent filled with the heat and smell of our encounter. Though it had chased every bit of chill out of the air, we'd still fallen asleep wrapped each other's arms as if we knew by morning it would be cold again.

The Third Day

Present

IN THE MORNING, WHEN I woke with her still lying naked in my arms, regret slammed through me. Not from the act itself. I fully admit, I enjoyed it more than I could have ever believed. It had been the wildest, most passionate love making I can ever remember having. Even with Hiyori, our few times having sex had been gentle, quiet, clean. With Yuna, we were grunting and moaning like half-crazed animals. I'd nearly torn her clothes in my need to feel her bare skin against me. Our bodies slapped together loud enough that I was certain someone heard us, though logically I know no one was around.

But I also knew that she had been a vulnerable girl, abused by two men in her life who she trusted, and here I was taking her like some animal. Beyond my brief hesitation, I didn't even spare much thought for how it could affect her mental and emotional well-being. Unlike those two, there were no years of pseudo-love and grooming to make her forgive me. I was already trying to figure out how to apologize, to atone so she wouldn't abort our deal and go off to finish her planned death when she yawned and stretched languidly against me.

Her smiling lips brushed mine. "Good morning!"

"Morning…" There was no sign she was upset but still, I tried to read into every movement as she sat up and stretched again. I gauged her every breath for some sign that I'd screwed up yet another person's life.

She looked back at me and shook her head. "You are so silly, Adachi. It's fine. It's what we both wanted." With a kiss and a giggle, she gathered her clothes and began dressing. "Bathroom and stream wash off?"

"Sorry. And yeah, that would be good." Half astonished, half bemused, I wondered if I would ever figure out how her mind worked, and if I did, would it somehow ruin some of the appeal she had?

We headed out of the tent and to our chosen bathroom spots for that camp. When I glanced back to see where she was, I was relieved to find she had moved her spot just a bit further away and was going at the same time instead of watching me like a hawk. While we did our stream cleanings together that was as much for practicality as anything else. It was too cold to linger long with water dripping from you, even if it was from just giving ourselves quick scrubs with dampened rags. As we had no buckets to move our washing water away from the stream itself, we didn't even use the all-natural soap Yuna had brought to avoid the chance of contaminating the water.

I was glad to see our night together seemed to have no ill-effects. If anything, Yuna acted even brighter and cheerier as we returned to camp and had our breakfast. Though we'd slept later that morning, it was still too early to head out into the woods. Besides, I already suspected yesterday had established the pattern: The nights were for her story, the mornings would be for mine. Even if it would be safe, I doubted she'd let us break camp until she had her turn listening to something from me.

As if on cue… "So, Adachi, will you tell me about her?"

That threw me. I thought for sure she'd demand to know about why I'd quit being a reporter now. "Her?"

"Yes, your girlfriend, or well, I guess ex-girlfriend now."

"What about her?"

"Everything. How did you meet? What did you like about her? Did you love her?"

"Oh…um…okay." I was still surprised that it was what she wanted to know, but a little relieved as well. Another reprieve from talking about the Nakamuras. "Hiyori-chan and I met in college during our first year. She was a pretty girl, tall with short hair cut in a bob. We had two classes together, English and history."

"Was she a journalism major too?"

"No, she was in linguistics, but first years often take a lot of the same basic classes. At first, she was just another classmate in a sea of faces. I didn't really notice her until one day when we happened to sit beside each other. Then I couldn't take my eyes off her. She was cute, smiling and shy whenever she looked at me. As class was ending, she dropped her book and I picked it up for her, which got us talking. After that, we sat together every class, talking before and after the lecture. It took me two weeks to work up the nerve to ask her out though."

Yuna's expression had an air of sadness, even wistfulness. Did she long to have that sort of regular romance? Had she ever known it before? "From there you started dating?"

"Yeah. We went out a few times then I asked if she wanted to be my girlfriend and she said yes."

"What did you like about her? I mean, other than that she was cute?"

"Hiyori-chan was smart, really smart, especially with languages. She was so good with English. I saw her help tourists sometimes, and even they seemed impressed by how good her English was. And she could speak, read, and write French and Spanish. She wanted to be an interpreter that worked internationally, so she was working hard to make herself an expert on multiple languages, trying to pick up all the ones she thought would be useful to give her flexibility and a high level of marketability. And she was a good person, kind and even-tempered."

"Are you saying she never got mad, not ever?" Her voice was heavily laced with skepticism.

"Not too often, no. We were together for five years. In all that time, I can only think of a few times she got really angry at anything." Of course, the last time had been the day she'd dumped me, furious at me for what I'd done. Most of the other times had been her angry at some injustice she'd seen or angry at someone other than me. Until that day, her anger had never really been directed my way.

"And you? Did you get angry?"

"Me? I...well, yeah, I guess. More than her, for sure,

though not at her. But things I'd read or learned about for stories sometimes made me angry and she'd always listen to me vent about it."

With an arched eyebrow, Yuna crossed her arms over her chest with a look of pure disbelief. "You never got angry at her? Not ever? Not even when she dumped you?"

"No, well, I mean…" I paused. The way she was looking at me, I knew she wouldn't be satisfied with a pat answer. In truth, I'd tried not to think about that day since it had happened. When I told her what happened and my part in it, she'd been angry then. She'd yelled and screamed at me, calling me all sorts of names before declaring we were through. "I don't know if angry is the right word. When we broke up, she was angry at me, and that hurt. I'd expected her to be disappointed, yes, but we'd been together five years! And she just dumped me, just like that, when I needed her support the most! I thought she loved me, but after she was gone and I realized that was it, she wasn't coming back, I started to think maybe she didn't really love me after all. I mean, do you just abandon someone you claim to love in the middle of a crisis because they screwed up?"

Yuna shook her head slowly. "Do you miss her?"

"I did at first, but not anymore. Maybe I didn't love her as much as I thought either." I replied slowly as the realization dawned on me. The first few weeks had been rough, but looking back on it now, it was more because I hated being alone and having to deal with everything by myself than her specifically I missed. I just wanted someone with me to tell me it would be okay, that I'd get through it all somehow. And when things had started clearing, I stopped thinking about her at all, until I came here, and even then, only in glancing. She sure as heck hadn't been in my mind at all the night before, when I'd let myself take what Yuna offered. "Five years together, and it meant so little?"

"I don't think it was a waste or anything, if that's what you're wondering. You were happy together until the end, right? You both got something out of it, it just wasn't meant to be forever, that's all." She shrugged. "So was that the only time that you ever got mad at her or that you two had a fight? Seriously, in five whole years?"

As if she had pulled it to the front of my mind, I remembered the one other time I'd been furious at her and we'd fought to the point of not speaking. "I think I mentioned my friend Shinji to you before?" After she nodded, I continued. "Well, we went to eat at his restaurant one day. I was so proud of what he'd done at his age and thought Hiyori would love it. But she was rude the whole time to him and his family, and after we got home, she laid into me about being around someone with such a 'disgusting lifestyle'."

"Disgusting lifestyle? I'm guessing he is gay or something?"

"Bisexual, actually." I found myself wanting to test her, to see if she was like Hiyori in that regard. "And he has both a husband and a wife, the three live together as a happy, wonderful, loving family."

"Oh, wow, that's amazing. I imagine it must be a little trickier, managing some parts of the relationship, but it sounds like he's been a good friend to you and that they are happy together. I guess your girlfriend viewed them the way most people would though." Yuna frowned and shook her head, almost too herself. "I'm sorry people can be so ugly like that sometimes."

"Thanks. It was hard talking to him the next time I saw him, I didn't know how to apologize. But the same guy she said was a pervert and a horrible human being said it was okay, they were kind of used to it and he knew it didn't reflect on how I felt too. And despite Hiyori never changing her views, he never once bad-mouthed her in front of me, always asked after her. He really is a great guy. I hope they are having the best vacation ever right now."

"Yeah, me too. He sounds like someone I'd like to meet one day." She grinned, then reached out and grabbed my hands. "Hey, let's go see the caves today!"

"The caves?"

"Yeah, you know, the ones up by the Northern entrance. You had to have seen them when you came in unless you walked in from the road. There is the Narusawa Ice Cave and I think one called the Wind Cave. They are a bit of a touristy thing, but they could be fun to see."

"Um, sure, though…" I must have looked confused because she smiled at me again.

"It's okay. I trust you to keep our deal."

Realizing she was right, at that point I don't think I could have brought myself to turn her in. Still, that she was telling me that left me feeling oddly touched and I kissed her forehead. "Thank you. Then yeah, let's go…though, um, how the heck would we get there?"

"No problem, we aren't too far from them. Just a bit north and west to get back to the path, then a short walk the rest of the way."

I looked for some sign her confidence in our location was just bravado or hubris, but she seemed sure. I had no idea how though, considering how much we wandered around the first two days. Still, even if she was wrong, it couldn't be that hard to find the path again. Worse case, we could walk until we found someone else's guide line, though I hated the thought of that option because following it the wrong way could lead to sights best left unseen.

"Okay, then, let's go," I replied as we crawled out of the tent, making up my mind that I would just enjoy the outing with her. Worst case, if I thought she was still going to go through with it, I had plenty of time yet to get help. As I grew more comfortable walking around with her, I also realized that I could now probably just catch her and tie her up if necessary when the seven days were over.

With that knowledge, I decided the best plan was to do just that, use the time to let her tell her story, to get to know her and get close to her. Then she wouldn't have to feel alone. She'd said she had no family or friends, right? So, again relying on my untrained counseling skills, it seemed logical to conclude that was why she was ready to die. But now she had a connection with me. If I could continue nurturing it, then she wouldn't go through with it and we could leave together, then maybe she could heal from her past and move on. Or at least that's what my ego wanted to believe.

To my astonishment, she did indeed lead us straight to the path within an hour or so. From there, we headed north, back the way I'd come. We were so close to the parking lot, I debated asking her if we could go check on my car, but I wasn't about to push things now and it was such a thin excuse it would be easy to see through. It wasn't like my car would get towed that fast.

So, I obediently followed her to the caves. Since they were all close together, it was easy enough to decide to see them all, starting with the ice cave known as Narusawa. They each had an entry fee, which explained her asking about money, though they were all cheap enough to not be a big hit on either of our wallets.

There was a small line to enter the cave, so we had to wait a bit. Yuna grew increasingly more excited as we got closer to our turn, to my delight and relief. When she was smiling and giggling, her attractiveness was difficult to ignore, and it was easier to tell myself I'd already fixed whatever had brought her here, and that things were fine. I'd keep my deal, we'd enjoy each other's company, and she would leave with me and all would be good.

"You know this cave is considered a geological wonder?" she asked as we moved forward another spot.

"Oh?"

"Yeah, it formed in year six of the Jogan era during an eruption of Mt. Fuji. The lava poured down the mount between two other volcanoes and formed this cave, along with many others. By the way, I hope you don't mind the cold. It's only like 4 or 5 degrees in there! The ice is present year-round, even in the heat of the summer, because it's under the mountain."

"The mountain itself doesn't melt it?"

"You'd think the heat would, but so far no one has observed it melting in recorded history."

As we stood in line, I noticed a few people looking at us in askance. Could they somehow sense the real reason we were in these woods? Or worse, did they recognize me? Were we going to have an ugly scene, like the last time I'd dared go out to get take out and was called a horrible person in public? Surely this place was too far away from my neighborhood to be recognized, especially the way I looked with my hair overgrown, stubble dirtying my chin.

"I just realized, we probably should have gone to the other place first, so we could clean up some," Yuna whispered, though her grin said she didn't care what people thought. Then it clicked, even with the stream baths, we were probably a bit dirty and unkept looking. I tried to sniff myself surreptitiously to see how bad it was, but that only elicited giggles from my traveling partner. "We smell fine, silly, no worse than other hikers anyway."

When it was finally our turn, we were led down the left fork of the steep steps that descended into the cave. As the people we'd seen earlier were coming up the other fork, I presumed the path circled around. The cave's entrance was a fascinating mix of the volcanic rock, the roots of the trees that would have hidden it had it been smaller, and moss blanketed it all. The stone steps were obviously man made, but still done in such a way they didn't feel that out of place.

As Yuna had warned, the further in we went, the lower the temperature dropped. Even with the exertion of going down the stairs, I found myself shivering at some spots. I thought we were already in the main part of the cave as we stopped to hear the guide talk about the history of the area and how the cave was formed. As she talked, we observed a set of historical artifacts: remnants of a silkworm seed storage area and an old well once used to pump out water from an underground aquifer.

After going around another curve, we found ourselves going down even more stairs, deeper underground. Another stop had us visiting a lava tunnel formed by the remnants of huge trees from over a millennium ago. I admit, I felt almost like a little kid oohing and ahhing over the site alongside an ecstatic Yuna. In the lit up parts around the cave, it was beautiful seeing how alive she had come and how much she enjoyed seeing everything. We ended up being the last of our group to leave every stop because she just didn't seem to want to tear herself away.

Around the next curve was an awesome wall made of ice blocks, recreating the old method of keeping food cool before refrigeration became a commonly available technology. Wrapping up the visit were cool ice stalactites, the only part of the cave to "melt", and even then, only from fall to the start of winter.

From there, we made the 800-meter or so walk to the other famous cave, the Fugaku Wind Cave. During the walk over, Yuna slipped her hand in mind so that we were walking together like any regular couple that didn't care if such public displays of affection were odd or frowned on. Her hand was small but warm in mine. The cave was like the first, except for the oddness of having no echo. We all took a try at getting an audible echo to come back to us, but due to the walls of the cave being so absorptive of sound, it was impossible! Yuna asked so many questions about the basaltic material that made the walls that even the guide was left unable to answer them all.

Once we were outside, I had to stretch the kinks out of my back. The cave had been much lower than the first one. Combined with the slippery service, I'd had to stoop over and walk with my muscles tensed much of the way. Still, I didn't mind at all. Maybe I was caught up in Yuna's enthusiasm, but I really enjoyed the experience. As we rested outside for a few minutes, I remembered our conversation that morning about Hiyori, then realized she would have hated this. She would have found the whole experience "distasteful" and dirty. She certainly wouldn't have crawled into the lava tube in the first cave, much less walked past the dripping walls without being grossed out, or allowed herself to hang on to strangers to catch each other as we slid around on the stairs together.

Then again, she'd have never come to these woods in the first place, or any woods. Camping wasn't an activity she would even remotely consider doing. While I hadn't gone in years myself, it was something I liked. And despite why I was there with Yuna, if I was being honest, I was enjoying it. Living in the woods, walking around and enjoying nature. It filled me with a sense of peace I hadn't felt since I was a teenager and had gone all the time.

"So, Adachi, what do you think? Did you enjoy that?"

"Yeah, yeah I did." I shared with her what I'd been thinking, except the part about truly accepting that Hiyori and I had been a poor match in many ways, and that I'd been more upset at being abandoned than losing a non-existent love.

"Good. I was worried you wouldn't because of why we're here, but it is nice, right? I think many people forget this forest has so much beauty and wonder in it. It all gets lost in the morbid reputation and the horror stories."

"Says the person who was planning to add to said reputation?" I was half teasing and half wondering if she would catch the past tense of my statement.

Yuna laughed. "True, true, I suppose I'm the last one to complain about it, considering my plans, but still, you'll remind people, right? It is part of our story now."

I told myself she also meant past plans, not future, and nodded. "It is indeed. And yeah, I will. Promise."

I thought I'd seen every one of her smiles, but the one

she gave me now was the brightest yet, so beautiful my heart flip-flopped in my chest. "It's a deal!"

The rest of the afternoon was spent walking more purposefully, in search of a spot to camp before it got too dark. We had two more retort meals for dinner. While they weren't the tastiest things, they weren't the worst things I'd eaten. Being a reporter could lead you to eating some very sketchy food while working a story and in need of a midnight meal because you hadn't eaten all day.

"By the way, these are our last two retorts. We'll be out of food after breakfast." She said it so casually it took a moment to register, but before I could panic, she continued. "So, I was thinking tomorrow we should visit Saiko Lake. We could camp near there and get some fishing in, or if we want to, we could even buy some food at the store there. We should have enough funds to get plenty for the rest of the week."

"Sounds like a plan." I had wondered if the lack of food would mean an early leaving, but I should have known better. If nothing else, Yuna seemed to have a thing about dealing and sticking to those deals. She reminded me of Taka, Shinji's husband. He was a businessman and, as such, put a lot of stock in each side keeping their part of a bargain. Though wasn't that normal human nature anyway?

We ate the meal as we had the others, in silence, though this time it felt more companionable than it had before. When we were done, I leaned back on my hands, staring up at the light hanging in the tent, letting my mind wander.

"Adachi?" Yuna's voice broke the half doze I'd slipped into.

"Hmm?"

"It's about time, isn't it?"

I almost said no, that I'd heard enough. I didn't want to know how much more she'd been hurt, what her breaking point ended up being, but at the same time, I knew I had too. Maybe that was really the subconscious thing that had driven me here: I needed to be here to get her story down because no one else had listened before.

"Yes, of course. Sorry, my mind was wandering a moment."

I grabbed my pen and notebook and we assumed our usual positions, me perched ready to write, legs crossed in front of me. Yuna always started sitting with her legs to the side, but I knew by the time she was done, she'd have shifted position multiple times, depending on her mood and what she was talking about. How many times would she change tonight, I wondered, then she began speaking…

End of Normalcy

AFTER THAT FIRST TIME in the woods, Akihito's appetite for his sister was unleashed and his so-called love grew only worse. In addition to regular trips to the woods, he would steal any moment he could to take her at their home. If their parents would be out of the house for enough predictable time, it was a given he would want to have sex with her.

Even though he was in college, he used the excuse of cutting down expenses and continuing to "help" his parents as his reason to continue living at home. In truth, he just wanted to continue his unfettered access to Yuna, so they could continue their "relationship."

As for Yuna, she would eventually come to realize that it was wrong, that brothers and sisters were not meant to be lovers, but by that point, it didn't matter to her any more than it did to him. For her side, how it began never really felt wrong, and that society considered it immoral meant nothing to her thanks to her heavy social isolation growing up. For she still loved her big brother, or at least per her understanding of love, and she'd come to crave the sex almost as much as he did. His corruption of her was total and complete, even as the terrible consequences for their actions circled ever closer.

If there was one strange spot in their life, it was that since the day Akihito had first had sex with her, she had not seen Noritaka again. When she tried to ask her brother about him, he'd gotten so angry and demanded she never even mention that name again. Sometimes she'd look around for him while walking to or from school. But if he was still walking with her brother, it was after they separated.

Her parents had also stopped mentioning him or discussing their engagement. After she finally tried asking her mother, the only response she got was that Noritaka's family had moved and had cut off all contact with them for reasons unknown. As such, the engagement was off. Yuna was left with no idea other than to wonder if Noritaka had gotten angry at her for telling Akihito about their forest activities and thus was punishing her by leaving her. He'd warned her it would happen and now it had.

Just over a year into her affair with Akihito, Yuna ran into his ex-girlfriend Kira. Kira had always seemed to like her and acted happy to see her.

"You doing okay, kiddo? Akihito behaving himself?" The phrasing was odd enough that Yuna did a double take.

"Um, yeah, I'm doing okay and I...I guess he is. I

mean…" She felt her cheeks grow hot as the image of him taking her that morning before breakfast came to mind unbidden. Somehow that wasn't likely to be considered behaving.

Kira sighed and shook her head. "I kept hoping he'd get over it, or at least wait until you were an adult. But from your expression, I'm guessing he revealed his feelings?"

"Yeah…wait, you knew?"

"Honey, we all knew." Kira laughed, but it was more self-derisive than unkind. "We all were just substitutes for you. Akihito, he…" But Kira broke off before finishing the thought. "Anyway, don't let him push you around, okay? You don't like it, say so and make him stop. And whatever you do, avoid getting pregnant, I know how he is about condoms."

"Okay, I'll try. Thanks." Yuna couldn't bring herself to dig anymore into what Kira meant by saying they had been substitutes. The part of her mind trying to preserve her safety to some degree didn't want to know, not then. "Oh, um, Kira, can I ask you something?"

"Sure, what's up?"

"You were friends with Noritaka too, right? Do you know why he left without a word?"

Kira's smile fell away and she looked uncomfortable a moment. "You really don't know?"

"No, no one will tell me anything, and Akihito forbade me say his name around him again."

"Look, kid, I'm not sure if it's right to tell you or not, but well, it was about you so I guess you should know. After Akihito found out about Noritaka messing around with you, he attacked him, damn near beat him to death."

Yuna's gasp filled the short pause before Kira continued. "Noritaka never told his parents or the police who attacked him, though his parents probably had a good idea since he didn't fight back. Not that I blame him, if he'd told it was Akihito, he'd have had to explain why he was attacked."

"What do you mean?"

"Well, because…you really don't realize it, do you, kid? I swear those boys…look, I'm sorry, Yuna, okay? I realized it long ago, but I let myself think I could change your brother because we got along so well, but I couldn't and, I don't know, I feel like there was more I should have done for you." Kira hugged her tight a moment. "I gotta go, but you stay safe, okay. And listen, Yuna, don't trust Akihito is right about everything, trust your own heart too. You're a smart kid, smarter than you think. You'll figure it all out."

Before she could reply, Kira had crossed the street just before the light changed, and moved away at such a fast pace, Yuna would have had to run to catch up to her. And at that point, Yuna was too shaken to run, still trying to picture her brother hurting his best friend. Had he been so jealous of Noritaka's attentions towards her?

Guilt ate her. She should have known better. He'd told her so many times that she was his special girl, it just hadn't occurred to her that it included being allowed to touch her. He'd let Noritaka hug her before, but still, she should have checked with him about the rest much sooner. She hated knowing Noritaka was hurt because of her and wished she could find him to apologize for her mistake. But for now, she knew all she could do was pray for his happiness and that he'd recovered from his injuries okay.

As for her, she and Akihito continued as they were, with her living in ignorance thanks to being friendless and isolated except for him, and her never realizing how much he was controlling and abusing her. And he continued to delude himself that his love for her was the purest, most wonderful thing ever, and that he was making her happier than anyone else possibly could. Then, a few weeks before Akihito turned 20, their parents came home early one late afternoon and found their older son naked and unmistakably having sex with his fifteen-and-a-half-year-old sister.

Just as one might expect in most families, the discovery brought about much yelling, screaming, and accusations. Alas, as noted, their parents had placed Akihito on a nearly untoppable pedestal, so it was not he who was yelled at, nor he who bore the brunt of the accusations. It was Yuna, innocent, violated, abused Yuna, whose parents called her a slut, a whore, a monster. So desperate was their need to keep their son as favorite that they immediately concluded that somehow Yuna had seduced and forced her older brother into such a situation out of jealousy.

And Akihito, for all his claims of love and devotion, for all his promises that their love was true and pure and good, did nothing to protect his sister, his proclaimed lover. He stood there unspeaking as her parents verbally assaulted her, declining to defend her or to confess his part in things. Instead, as soon as his father noticed him still there and ordered him out, Akihito had bolted to his bedroom, changed clothes, and ran out of the house to go to his part-time job early!

Yuna was left with her parents reddened faces, screaming and berating her at length. Even as they demanded she get dressed, they were keeping such a steady barrage going the task took three times as long as it normally might have. At this point, she'd known that having sex with her brother was wrong, but the things they yelled made no sense. That she'd seduced him? That he hadn't wanted it? But he'd been the one who'd touched her first, right? He said he needed her, that he loved her, that it had to be her and only her. So why were they acting like she was the only one to blame and why had he left her alone to deal with them?

In the end, their reasoning for blaming her, or lack thereof, resulted in her being shoved into the car with her father with her purse and phone in hand and a small bag with her clothes and basic toiletries she was ordered to pack at her feet. He drove for a long time, and after she was told not to even speak to him, Yuna gave up and eventually dozed off, exhausted from the drama of the day.

When she woke, it was dark and her father was pulling up beside a busy street in a brightly lit area, full of neon and moving boards. The car was still rocking to a stop when he leaned over and pushed the door open.

"Get out, you whore." Confused, and scared, Yuna complied. Her father threw the bag out at her and gave her one last contemptuous look. "You're dead to us. Don't bother us again and stay the hell away from our son."

As she watched, her father screeched back into traffic and drove out of her life. Yuna was too shocked to even call after him. The place she found herself in was full of people, lights, and so many buildings. It made even downtown Nagano look pedestrian and quiet. Realizing some people were staring and pointing at her while whispering behind their hands, Yuna pulled herself from her trance, grabbed her bag, and walked down the road to try to figure out where she was. The bustling crowds were difficult to navigate at first, and the constant stream of traffic was unnerving.

Two blocks later, she stopped to stare in wonder at the sign of JR Shinjuku Station's south gates. The train station was bigger than any she had ever seen, but its impressiveness was lost on the fact that her father had driven over three hours to dump her in Tokyo! Deciding to take stock and figure out what she should do next, she ducked into the small Krispy Kreme nearby. To avoid being kicked out for loitering she got a small coffee and, realizing she hadn't eaten in hours, a berry jelly stars donut.

Once she had her order and was seated in a back corner out of the way, she carefully counted all the money in her purse. It wasn't much, since she didn't get the same spending money as Akihito and, as she hadn't planned on being dumped, she wasn't as frugal with it as she could be. Minus the change from her meal, she had exactly fifteen thousand yen left. It would only just barely cover a train ticket back home. A bus would be cheaper, but was there any point in going tonight? Would her parents have calmed down enough to let her come home, or had they meant what they said about her never coming back?

She checked her phone messages, but there was not a single call from Akihito. Why? Why hadn't he called? It had been over three hours since they were discovered, surely by now he knew what had happened at home? But wait, no, he would still be at work. She doubted her parents would call him there to tell them.

For now, it seemed prudent to her to just wait. Once Akihito came home and found out, he'd call her and tell her where to wait for him and then he'd come get her. Meanwhile, she should probably make herself look at least somewhat more presentable, so people would quit staring. She headed into the cafe bathroom to straighten her hair and change into slightly less rumpled clothes from her bag, glad she had that much at least.

By her estimate, she had two hours to wait until Akihito would get home from work, and it would take at least three hours for him to reach her there. She decided to look for a manga cafe to wait in, as it would be cheaper to sit there for hours and she could get something else to eat. The donut had been delicious, but she was already hungry again.

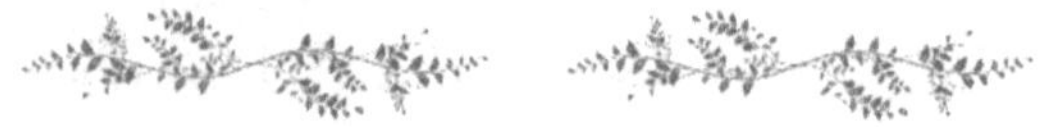

THE TIME WHEN AKIHITO should have been home from work, and learned what her parents had done, came and went. Still her phone didn't buzz with a text message, email, or voice mail. No familiar ring tone that he was calling. Nothing at all. The cafe staff had started giving her looks after an hour or so, so she'd left and wandered the station, looking in the various shops as if she was a normal teenager just hanging out after school. Instead of a potentially homeless one dumped with no resources or no idea what to do next.

Tired of waiting, Yuna ducked into a quiet spot of the station and called Akihito's number herself. It rang twice then clicked as if someone had picked up, but immediately disconnected again. Had he just hung up on her? No, must have been an accident. When he didn't immediately call back, she tried again. "This call cannot be completed as the receiver has blocked this number. Thank you and have a good day."

Yuna stared at her phone in shock for a minute. He'd blocked her number? Akihito was fine with things like this? It had to be a mistake. Akihito was supposed to come save her, he loved her, she was his most precious person, his one and only girl. So why… why was he not calling? Why had he ignored her?

Hot tears ran down her cheeks as she realized she was well and truly abandoned. But she wasn't even old enough to get a job, much less an apartment or register herself for school. What was she supposed to do now? She viciously swiped at her eyes and sniffed. Damn him, damn him to hell. Damn her whole family. She hadn't done anything wrong, she'd tried to be a good daughter, a good sister, and this was her reward?

Whatever, first things first, she needed time to figure out what she wanted to do. And with the hour growing later, a safe place to stay for the night. There seemed to be a lot of hotels north of the station, so she headed that way first. If nothing else, she should be able to find a capsule hotel for a price she could afford. It wouldn't be the most comfortable option, but at least it would be safe, quiet, and give her time to think.

The first places she looked at were all male only, but finally she spotted one with a sign indicating it was specifically for women! The price was right, too, at less than 3,000 yen, especially after she pulled up i-mode and found a coupon to use. She'd already decided to claim she had missed her train back home to Nagano, but doing that would mean waiting until after 10 pm to check in. With an hour to wait, she noted exactly where it was and carefully retraced her steps back to a park she'd passed earlier and perched on a fountain not far from some other girls her age. She figured if they looked so comfortable out there that time of night, it must be a safe enough place to sit for a bit.

After a few minutes she noticed they would get approached by random guys, usually older. Rather than blow them off, the girls would smile, be friendly, and then often leave with one. Pretending to be busy with her phone, she eavesdropped on one such meeting that happened near her. The guy approached a cute girl, offering her ten thousand yen if she would go do karaoke with him. All giggles and smiles, the girl accepted and they left together. Seriously, that girl just made ten thousand yen by going and having fun with a decent enough looking guy for a few hours!?

With so little time spent with others, one thing Yuna had done was read, a lot. Manga, especially, but fortunately it covered this situation. She realized the girls must be engaging in the trade known as enjo kōsai. From what she read, it was basically getting paid to go on dates. The dates often didn't even involve sex, so it wasn't like prostitution, though girls did sometimes do sex-related activities too, if they wanted. People looked down on girls who did it, but the girls got money to spend on expensive, brand name goods, were often spoiled by their clients, and had fun. When they had enough or got too old, they just stopped.

It wasn't something she'd ever seen happening in Nagano, though she wasn't often out at night back home either. While randomly checking her phone and acting as if she was waiting for someone, she continued to watch the girls working. There were about half a dozen in the area that seemed to be casually "hanging" out, looking to pick up dates. It was interesting how similar the guys' approaches were, even for different dates, though a few would be vague about how they wanted to spend time. They and the foreigners seemed to get turned down the most. Two girls were even bold enough to approach potential guys themselves. She wondered if one of them was newer, as she seemed to strike out more on finding guys of interest. The other one was very good at spotting a guy who'd say yes and had just been too shy to approach a girl first.

Now and then one would glance over at Yuna, but she made sure to act completely uninterested in anything but her phone, as if she was waiting for someone. When it was finally ten, she headed back to the capsule hotel. With her sob story of missing her last train after coming to check out a potential college, she had no trouble getting checked in, especially since she had the funds to pay.

Her stomach reminded her that one donut did not a meal make. After taking a quick shower and changing into the hotel yukata she'd been given when she checked in, she headed down to the snack bar to find something to eat. She was torn on what to get, considering how much money she had left, but in the end, she knew she needed to eat more or she'd just be hungry again later, so she got a bowl of ramen for 1000 yen. The hotel had a manga corner, so she grabbed a couple of volumes to read while she ate.

Settled in her capsule with the shade down, she flicked the television on to the news, then grabbed the notebook out of her bag and tried to think. She had dwindling funds, at best she could do one more night in a hotel like this before being broke. First things first, in the morning she'd try her parents and Akihito again. Most likely they would have calmed down by morning. If not, she'd try her aunt and grandparents next. They could talk to her parents and straightening things out, surely…

"Wishing won't get us anywhere," she said aloud to herself. The chances of her being allowed back home were slim to none. "Get it together, Yuna, we're on our own now. We have to figure out what to do." After plugging her phone into the charger, she pulled up i-mode again to access the area job database to see if there were any jobs someone her age could do, making notes in the notebook as she went. A few restaurant positions, cafes, and the like. Most wanted 16 though, and she wasn't quite there yet. Plus there was the issue of pay; most of them didn't pay enough to cover even one week's worth of living, if today was any indication, much less a month.

A place to live required funds, funds required a job, a job that paid decently. She wasn't really wanting to stay in a capsule hotel every night, but it was an easy enough option, that and love hotels. Both were pretty affordable, private, and at least with the latter, she could generally check in and have her own room without having to see anyone else. Those would be a better option than the capsule hotel and more comfortable.

She estimated 3-8,000 yen a night for the hotel, since worse case a capsule was better than nothing. Probably another 5-6,000 more for food. Then there were clothes and the like. Yuna's sigh filled the capsule. Even the best part-time job wouldn't pay nearly enough; at best it would help with food and spending money. And something legitimate that was full-time would be almost impossible to get at her age.

She thought back to the girls she'd seen earlier. They were making well over that a night just going out and having fun. But could she? Akihito and Noritaka had known her all her life; would strange men find her cute and want to spend time with her? She decided there would really be only one way to find out for sure, first thing tomorrow evening.

IN THE MORNING, YUNA checked her phone for messages, emails, anything from Akihito. Nothing. She tried calling again and was again told her number was blocked. She called home, but the phone said it was disconnected. Then she tried her grandparents, who hung up on her after calling her a whore. Her aunt didn't even say anything at all. There seemed little point in trying any other relatives she could think of. Tears formed in her eyes, but she refused to let them fall. She'd already cried, and more wasn't going to change the situation. It was time to admit she was on her own. Akihito had abandoned her along with the rest of her family. Which meant finalizing her plans and putting them into action.

Finding her first date would have to wait till evening, since that seemed to be the best time for random pickups. Meanwhile, she went to the various jobs she'd found in the ads to see about a part-time job. As she expected, most said she was too young, should go home (having decided she was a runaway), or both. By lunch time, she was tired of walking around and being rejected. While eating an inexpensive curry lunch, she wished she had thought to grab her bank book when she was kicked out. Not that she'd been expecting to be kicked out, but something to keep in mind in the future. Always be prepared for such things.

She spent the afternoon at the public library, researching enjo kōsai and firming up her plans. First, she made her best estimates of what her living expenses would be. She already had the basic list from the night before, which made it go faster. The hotels would be expensive after a while, but it also saved her on any utilities and the fees needed to get an apartment, not that anyone would be likely to rent one to her without parental support.

To successfully date, she would need more than the two outfits she had now and it would be nice to have her own toiletries. Plus supplies for that time of the month, things like that. And a way to carry it all and store it. For now, it would have to be the train station lockers, which would be safe enough, though it added to the expenses too.

Still, if she was calculating it all correctly, and going by what she'd seen last night, two dates a night just might be enough for her to live on, as long as she didn't go crazy with spending money. After all, she didn't care about designer purses and jewelry; she just needed food, shelter, and her work supplies. She laughed under her breath. "Work supplies" indeed.

She went back to the same place she'd seen the other girls the night before, sat a little apart from them, and did her best to look bored and waiting. Less than a minute later, a man walked up to her and said hello. Remembering all the things that Akihito and Noritaka had liked her to do, she smiled and greeted him warmly. He was a little taller than Akihito, with his straight dark hair in a short, tousled style. He had a nice-looking face, though, and a lean, trim body.

"Waiting for your boyfriend?" he asked, his smile showing his white, even teeth.

"Nope." She shook her head with a pout, deciding to play up the abandoned angle. "To be honest, I got dumped here and now I'm all on my own."

"Dumped? That's horrible." He laid his hand on her arm, which she took as a good sign. "Would you like to have dinner with me? I was looking for a little company as I hate eating alone. You can tell me all about being dumped, my treat. I'll even pay you for putting up with listening to this old man blab if you like, say ten thousand yen?"

"Thank you, that sounds nice." She wrapped her arm around his. It didn't matter that he was almost twice her age, and at least the first one she snagged was a nice-looking guy.

He introduced himself as Hoji as he led the way to a casual restaurant not far from where they met. She appreciated it, since she was just wearing her school uniform and would have been out of place in a fancy place. The food was good, and she'd enjoyed her time with him. Hoji turned out to be a manager in a large company who worked a lot. He had a hard time dating because women got fed up with his lack of time for them. He'd talked to Yuna on a whim and it was only his second time trying compensated dating.

He had a nice voice, seemed kind, and had lovely manners. During the dinner, he hadn't just talked about himself, but had asked about her too, mostly just casual questions. Sometime during the conversation, they'd gotten back around to being her being dumped in Shinjuku.

"My parents caught me having a bit of fun with my brother's friend and blew their lid. My dad drove me all the way here and dropped me off, said never to come home again. I don't get why they got so mad, we weren't hurting anything you know?"

"Oh, that is terrible. That seems like such an overreaction. I hope they will call you soon and come pick you up. Meanwhile, what will you do for tonight? Do you have a place to sleep?"

"I have a little money on me at least, so I was thinking I'd get a room at one of the hotels here or that place by the train station that looked pretty cheap. With the automated systems I won't have to worry about my age being an issue. A hostel might ask too many questions, you know, and I'm so not wanting to go to one of those places."

"True and I don't blame you at all. But those hotels you mentioned are not very good places for a nice girl like you. Tell you what, I know a place not too far from here. I stay there sometimes if I'm out late and miss the last train home. I'll get you a room there, if that's okay." He gasped then waved his hands in front of him as if embarrassed. "Wait, that sounded wrong. I don't mean for that, I promise. I just hate to think of you in some sketchy place. I won't even go near the room."

"Are you sure? I hate to put you out." She made sure to add a tone of uncertainty, not wanting to seem too eager. Not that she had any issue with going to the places she'd scoped out, but if he was going to pay, she wouldn't have to use her money right away. His expression seemed genuinely concerned and sympathetic. He was a decent looking guy, though, if she ended up having to do something extra to get the room, it wouldn't be that bad, though she'd prefer to keep the first date platonic.

"Yes, it will be my pleasure. Shall we go?"

As they'd finished eating anyway, she agreed. The hotel was indeed nice, much nicer than the places she'd have been able to afford, even with the money he'd even given her before they'd gone to the hotel in case she got too nervous and changed her mind. Once they had the key, she assured him she was fine if he came up to check out the room, so he did.

She bounced on the soft bed. "Thank you again, Hoji-san. This is really nice of you."

"No problem. I'm glad I could help." He stayed standing, seeming to be careful not to come too close to the bed. "It's getting late, so I should probably go. Um…Yuna-chan, if it's okay with you, could I have your number? If you do end up staying, I'd love to spend time with you again."

"Oh, sure. I'd like that too." She walked over so she could send it to his cell. After that he'd ruffled her hair and advised her to get a good night's sleep, then left. She still couldn't believe he'd actually given her the room without wanting any kind of sex at all, but she certainly wasn't complaining.

A long soak in the tub sounded divine, but first she needed to hang out her virtual shingle for business. From her earlier research, she already knew which site she wanted to use, so she logged in and registered herself as being available for dating. It would be easier to get dates, even in the daytime, if she was on-line in a system, as a lot of men felt less than comfortable just walking around trying to pick out which girls were looking for dates and which were just walking alone. It also let her get the pricing part out of the way, as she could list her rates, at least for the non-sexual stuff. If that came up, she had rates in mind too, but it didn't pay to advertise those.

With that done, she headed off to relax in the tub, hoping they would have some bubbles she could add to the water.

Present

I'm NOT SURE HOW I managed to continue writing my notes as I listened to Yuna. As appalled as I was at her brother's raping of her, her parents' abandonment had been the last thing I had expected. Sure, it had been clear they were as obsessed with their son as perfection as their son was obsessed with Yuna, but still, nothing else had indicated they could so easily throw their child away without even a moment's hesitation.

Yuna reached out and wiped the tears away from my face that I hadn't realized had fallen. Her voice was soft and gentle, and rather than pity I saw only affection and concern in her expression. "You really are too kind to be a reporter, Adachi. Should we stop here?"

A sharp pain speared through me at her well-meaning

words. I didn't deserve it, not with what I'd done. I was tempted to tell her right then all about the Nakamuras, how I'd murdered them, why I was such a horrible human being. But even then I held back, rationalizing that if she wanted to know, she'd ask during one of my morning sessions, though of course she didn't know about it to ask, which was fine.

"Ah, no, sorry. I didn't even realize…" I covered her hand in mine. "I'll be okay, I promise. I need to know the rest, please."

"Okay then, but that's all for tonight. We both could use a break." She leaned up to brush a kiss over my lips. The heartache I felt for her threatening to overwhelm me, I reached for her greedily, drinking from her to ease the wounds that should rightfully be hers. I made love to her in the same way, desperate to stop the pain and hoping somewhere inside it was soothing whatever hurt she must be hiding inside from recounting her parents' cruelty.

Later, as we lay sated and Yuna had dozed off snuggled against me, holding me tight as she seemed to, I let myself think back on today's section. With the initial emotional reactions calmed, I realized it wasn't entirely surprising. It was only this year that Akihito's actions would have even been considered rape by the authorities, as he hadn't been violent or forced her, only groomed her. And her parents' response was in-line with many people's views of rape and sexual abuse, particularly among family. It was always the girl's fault; she was the horrible "whore" who must have seduced the male. Society was finally coming around and getting in touch with reality, but it was a slow process and such aging attitudes were taking too long to die off for my taste.

I couldn't help admiring her resourcefulness in the situation she found herself in. To not even be sixteen but able to come up with a tentative survival plan, deal with lodging, budget her funds, and even find ways to make money. Granted, I was less comfortable knowing she had done so starting in the enjo kōsai scene, but I couldn't fault her logic. One could make far more money than at any part-time job a teenager could get, especially one under sixteen, and it wasn't as if she hadn't tried the regular job route too.

Still, as much as I hated hearing what happened, I'd been honest when I told her I had to know the rest. Some part of me wished she hadn't fallen asleep or decided to stop there, so great was my need to hear more of her story. Her parents and her brother's actions would certainly have been enough to drive someone to consider suicide, but seven years later? When she hadn't cried or looked sad recounting those events, other than a few tears when she talked of realizing Akihito had abandoned her? What else happened after that, what had been her final straw? I had to know.

The Fourth Day

Present

IN THE MORNING, WHEN I woke, Yuna was still asleep. As I lay in the quiet of the early morn, watching her sleep, I felt something in me shift. My original desire to stop her suicide had everything to do with myself, with not wanting to be a murderer again. But now, looking at her snuggled up against me, her hair blanketing my still-sleeping arm that she'd used as a pillow, I simply wanted her to live. Her specifically. I wanted to protect her, nurture her, know more about the quirky things that made her laugh, her fascination with the caves, why she had so much camping gear. I wanted to know how she looked if she struck out at bowling or how she'd cheer if she made a strike.

I wanted her to leave that forest with me at the end of our week, but I also wanted her to stay with me, to leave with me, not just walk out and go on her way back to whatever life she'd almost left behind. Perhaps some part of it was the age-old need to be a hero, wanting to be her knight in shining armor who would come to love and cherish her the way she truly deserved, rather than just use and abuse her. Somehow, in just three days, I knew she was someone I'd been missing in my life without even realizing it, someone I needed in my life and had to keep there.

It wasn't that I completely forgot why we were there, it was still in the back of my mind, but I left it there. Instead, I was focusing on enjoying my time with her as much as I could while recording her story and picturing us reading the resulting articles together, her praising me over how I phrased something. And yes, at that moment, I'd also put aside the fact that I'd already tried to quit the paper, and had every intention of doing so when I went home, that I wasn't a reporter anymore. Just as she had when she'd accepted my offer to record her story.

Our relationship was built on a deal and lying to ourselves, and I didn't care. I just knew with her I felt at peace again, and other than the nightmares, I was going hours at a time without thinking of the Nakamuras. Part of me felt guilty for it, as if I'd forgotten them and why I'd come there myself. During those moments, I'd sometimes slip out the article to look at their picture again, to remind myself that this happiness I was feeling was not for monsters like me, not for a murderer. That my only job was to fix her up and send her on her way, then get back to why I was there, to make amends with the Nakamuras.

That morning was the first time Yuna let me go to the bathroom on my own, trusting I would return. She even sent me off to the nearby stream to refill our water bottles while she worked on putting things away and getting breakfast together. I felt certain these were strong signs that she was already feeling better and would leave at the end of the week, alive and ready to get back to her life. After all, if she still wanted to die, she surely wouldn't let me out of her sight like that, too afraid I'd summon the authorities somehow to come get her. Not that I could if I wanted to, since I had no phone, but I wasn't sure if she believed me when I said I didn't.

As I returned to the campsite with the water, I felt a familiar feeling of dread welling up. Today would be the day I'd be forced to talk about the Nakamuras, I was sure of it. I'd have to explain it all, then hope she still had any interest in me at all. I still didn't want to talk about it, but when she'd shared so much at this point, I had no right to keep it to myself. As we settled in the tent to wait out the morning darkness, I braced myself for the question: Why are you no longer a reporter?

"Okay, Adachi, this morning, will you tell me about your family?"

"Huh? My…my family?" I asked as a mix of relief and disappointment coursed through me.

"Yeah, you know the parentals, siblings, those folks." She laughed as she teased me. "Was your family close? Where are you from, what was your childhood like, stuff like that."

"Oh, uh, sure. Let's see…well, I'm the middle child in my family. My sister Chika is two years older than me and my brother Fumio is three years younger. We get along pretty well, other than the usual sibling squabbles." I said it without thinking, then realized that maybe for Yuna, even what seemed mundane and ordinary might be unusual to her. "We'd argue over silly things, like toys and stuff when we were kids, and teased each other a lot when we were older. But we were always there for each other if things got rough."

"How so?"

"When my sister's husband decided to leave her after just five years for his secretary, she had a hard time of it. Older people especially can be cold towards single mothers, even if they are single through no fault of their own. They won't rent them places, gossip about them, won't hire them for jobs, crap like that. But Fumio found her an apartment in a nice neighborhood and quietly made an agreement with the landlord to secretly pay half the rent so she could afford it. I used my connections to help her find a job. We also kept 'accidentally' ordering too much food the numerous times we'd 'randomly' drop in for dinner, so she'd have left overs. She finally caught on after almost a year, but by then she was back on her feet so we got done what needed to get done."

"Ah. So where did you guys do your squabbling?"

"I'm originally from Hakodate. We lived in a neighborhood right between Mount Hakodate and the coast, in the Aoyagicho district. I grew up playing in the woods and loved it. In the summer, we could go to the beach almost every day. My parents were never rich, but we weren't poor either. They made decent incomes and were able to give us a comfortable life without spoiling us. I can't think of a time we wanted for anything. We had a small, but comfortable two-story house there with a small backyard, just big enough to relax in."

"Did you have a lot of friends in school?" She asked.

"Yeah, I guess I did. There was a group of us that hung out together a lot, going to the mall or just wandering around. Most of us went to the same elementary, middle, and high schools. You'd think after all those years together, it would have made us the best of friends, but after we all graduated, I lost touch with most of them. Only one or two I regularly keep in touch with these days." Really, it was just Shinji. While a few classmates had even called me just to condemn me, he'd called to ask how I was and offered me a place with him and his family if I needed a place to just regroup for a while.

Yuna sighed softly. "That's how people are, I think. We can be so close to each other when we're together like that, in school or at a job. We talk about anything and everything, share secrets, the whole deal. We have best friends and all. But then, as soon as that connection is gone and we no longer have that regular interaction, all of that just goes away and becomes meaningless. We forget and then look back when we're older and wonder what happened to this person or that person." She crossed the small space between us to nestle between my legs, snuggling against my chest.

I wrapped my arms around her as if it were the most natural thing in the world. For a brief moment, it was if we were just a regular couple having a nice conversation. Her words rung all too true, sadly, and matched my own experiences. "You know, I once interviewed a guy who was doing studies on the relationships we have in our lives and he'd said something similar. That his research showed human relationships really need that regular contact; without it, we seem to just stop remembering what made us like each other. He thought it might be a biological de-fense mechanism, like how if someone dies, you slowly heal and things you did together become a distant memory, allowing you to move on with your life."

"Hmmm…that kind of makes sense in a way. If we spent all our time moping about the people who aren't around us anymore, it would be hard to function. Though it does make it sad too. It's probably why long-distance relationships are so hard to keep going, because I think love works the same way. Without that regular together-ness, there isn't much to hold you together but your feel-ings, and those are so easily swayed." Her last bit had a tinge of sadness to it, no doubt from her own experiences with the flaky pseudo-love of her abusers and family.

I kissed the top of her head and held her a bit longer, content to sit just like this. Part of me would have been happy to spend our remaining time together like that, snuggled together, making love as the mood struck, and just enjoying being together. I knew it wasn't practical though, and I suspected she would just balk at the notion anyway. I wanted to ask her how she'd come to have her camping skills and what not, but I was sure that would come during the rest of her story.

"Shall we go to the lake?" she asked even as she tight-ened her arms around me and leaned up to plant little kisses along my jaw line. "We can take a shower and stuff and maybe get some more food."

"Sure, that does sound good."

While we'd splashed some water from the streams on our faces in the morning, we hadn't really bathed since we got there. With the low temps, we weren't sweating a lot during our hiking, but our night activities certainly had worked up the heat more. After doing our usual pack up, we checked our direction on the compass and headed out. As before, Yuna seemed to find her way without having to check the compass too often and it never once felt like we'd gotten turned around or gone anything but relatively straight there.

It only took an hour or so to reach the shore from where we'd camped. We came out near one of the parking spots for the lake where one or two cars sat waiting for their owners' return. As soon as she saw the water, Yuna squealed and ran across the road and down the stairs to stand on the thin strip of shore on that side.

A moment later her hair was unbraided and blowing in the light breeze, dancing around her face. When she looked towards me as I joined her, I was struck speechless by how beautiful she looked in that moment, a sweet smile playing on her lips and her face aglow with her happiness. Even though I had been with her the last few days, with the low light in the forest and the intense vibrancy of all the greens, it had given her a kind of muted appearance, much like she probably saw me. This was my first time truly seeing her in full living color and I was awed. It was easy to see now how she'd so quickly picked up her first dates.

Wordlessly, we turned and walked along the shore a bit, her leading while holding my hand as I followed behind her. It was perhaps one of the most wonderful moments of my life, though it was so plain and almost ordinary. Yet it stuck with me so clearly, the sounds, the smells, and the feel of her slender hand in mine. I felt like a strong man, holding that little hand, as if I could protect her from the horrible world that had treated her so badly. The water had done strange things to my mind.

The slip of a shore soon petered out, so we got back on the road and walked another three kilometers or so until we reached the Saikokohan Camping Grounds. We'd originally planned to do just use one of the day rental options so we could take showers, but we discovered they had a few of the 4.5 tatami cabins available. It didn't take much convincing for us to decide to rent one, especially as we were able to get a small discount that allowed us to also check out some equipment for cooking. It was much more expensive than the day passes would be, but we were both fine with doing it as sleeping inside for one night would be worth it.

"Mmm, I don't mind the tent, but this will be heavenly!" Yuna said as she dropped her bag in the cabin and spun around the room.

The cabins had beautiful wood sides and one large screened in set of double doors on one side offering a nice view outside. The bed was basic and relatively small, but right then it looked like the most luxurious thing in the world. I hadn't realized how sick I was of sleeping on the ground until I'd seen it. I was already looking forward to tonight.

Once we'd put our gear away, we made a quick trip to the store on site and bought stuff for today's lunch and dinner, and more instant meals that would be usable for when we went back out to the woods tomorrow. We stored all but the lunch foods in the cabin then headed down to the lake to play in the water and walk along the shore some more. As with our time walking through the forest, our walking the shore was mostly quiet, enjoying each other's company. Any conversation we did have was mild, banal. I think between her story and mine, we needed the mental break during the day to just talk about small, inconsequential things or enjoy a companionable silence.

We ate lunch on the shore and walked a bit more before turning around and heading back. As if to make us extra glad we'd chosen that day to go to the camp grounds, it started to rain while we were walking. It started as just a light mist, but we picked up the pace just in case. By the time we got back just before dusk, the rain had stopped, but the weather forecast predicted rain the rest of the evening so we went ahead and took our showers and made our dinners in the available shared kitchen area before settling into our cabin for the night.

Dinner was slower than usual, with us both enjoying the luxury of eating inside and with full lighting instead of the softer glow of the tent light. In a strange way, it was as if we were eating together for the first time again and both acted almost shy and uncertain at first. But eventually the routine we'd established reasserted itself and soon were sitting on the bed, facing each other, my pen poised over my notepad waiting to see where things went next with her life.

Enjo Kōsai

EVEN YUNA WAS SURPRISED at how easy it was for her to get started with her new "career" in enjo kōsai. In the morning, after checking out from the hotel, she used some of the funds to get more clothes. It wouldn't do to keep wearing the same two outfits, especially if she managed to get regulars. She went for the sorts of clothes that Akihito and Noritaka tended to compliment the most, deciding if they had liked them, other men would too. From her research, she also knew that most men preferred their dates to act their age, rather than trying to dress or act older.

She was able to find a good secondhand store that had a nice selection, which helped with the budget. In the end, she picked up three skirts, two blouses, and one dress, along with a pair of cute shoes to go with them. By necessity, she also picked up some under clothes, basic toiletries, a new charger for her phone, as she'd left hers at her former home, and a sturdy tote bag to carry her things in.

With the shopping done, she kept wearing her older outfit until it was closer to work time. No point risking it getting damaged or dirty early. The new clothes and other items were stored in the bag, which she stowed in one of the lockers in the train station, keeping just her phone and purse. Without the weight to carry around, she spent the rest of the day exploring the area, finding good date spots in case guys needed ideas, and trying to get a feel for places that might be a bit sketchier and that she should avoid.

As evening approached, she went back to the station to change into one of her new outfits before stowing the bag again, then logged into the board to see if anyone was looking for dates or had requested her. No requests, but plenty of guys were already starting to post. The first she clicked on was a 23-year-old wanting several cute girls to join him and some other friends for a big private party. While groups weren't unusual, something about the post made her feel uneasy. Trusting her instincts, she skipped and checked another. Twenty-two-year-old looking for a cute girl to go to a movie with him. He'd even listed the title of the film, a sentimental, romantic one about star-crossed lovers who somehow connected across time to meet one another. It was one Yuna had wanted to see too, and she could understand why the guy wanted someone to go with him since it wasn't a "guy" sort of film. So she responded with an offer and soon the deal was done. 8,000 yen and he was buying the movie tickets.

They met in front of the theater. Hayate was a large,

muscular guy, not gorgeous, but not hideous either. He had such a bright grin, it made up for his homelier features, and he was polite from the moment they met, thanking her profusely for being willing to go with him. He confessed he loved these kinds of movies, but it was embarrassing going alone and asking female friends would probably cause misunderstandings.

The movie was as good as they both hoped and they cried together at the emotional ending, then laughed at each other as they left. Afterward, they talked a bit outside the theater. Before they parted ways, he asked if he could call her again for more movies and she gladly agreed. It was an easy way to earn money and see movies she liked. The conversation flowed nicely too, which was a bonus. She suspected it would be easier talking to guys she could find something to genuinely like about them versus having to completely fake it.

She checked the boards again and found another client that seemed like a good one. He wanted a dinner companion, like Hoji had, except he was seventy-years-old. But his request specifically asked for someone with long red hair and emphasized it was purely a platonic dinner. With the outrageous 35,000 yen payment, plus the meal at an expensive restaurant, Yuna accepted and agreed to meet in an hour. It gave her just enough time to go back to the train station and change back into her school uniform, also per the request specifications.

The man reminded her a bit of her grandfather, who'd died five years before. He had a stooped appearance and all white hair, with a kind face. He looked particularly happy to see her wearing the school uniform. The man attending him smiled at her and gave her a quick bow, as if thanking her as well. They dined at the top floor of one of the higher end hotels, giving Yuna a chance to eat a higher caliber of food than she normally did. It took an effort to eat politely when her hungry body wanted to scarf the scrumptious food down.

He truly did seem to just want a platonic date, encouraging Yuna to chat normally about school stuff, movies, the sorts of things girls were into. So she told him about the movie she'd just seen and tried to remember the stuff she'd heard other girls her age chatting about in the square and at school. While Akihito hadn't allowed her to have friends, she'd enviously eavesdropped on their conversations, desperately wishing she could join in. Occasionally she had, but as soon as the girls realized she'd never hang out with them or go do things with them, they would drop her as they presumed she thought she was too good for them and other crap like that.

At the end of the date, the man hugged her with a broad smile and thanked her for making his evening more cheerful. He excused himself to use the bathroom and while he was gone, his companion explained about the date. The old man had a granddaughter he loved very much, one who had been about Yuna's age and who had long red hair. Every year for her birthday he treated her to a nice dinner as a present. But she'd died the year before. He hoped by treating another girl to dinner, it would help ease the pain the anniversary of her birthday had caused. The younger man thanked her himself before his boss returned, saying he was sure the girl would approve too.

Yuna didn't mind being a substitute and was glad it had made the old man laugh again instead of spending the night alone, bitterly regretting his losses. With the money from the old man, plus the 15,000 yen "tip" the companion had added, she decided she didn't need to do a third date that night. Besides, she suspected anyone looking at that hour would certainly want sex, and it seemed smarter to wait on doing those kinds of dates after she had a better knack for feeling out potential weirdos and knowing which hotels were good ones to use in case anything went wrong.

Instead, she headed to a late-night cafe to have a drink and figure out where she wanted to stay for the night. While waiting until it was closer to ten, she found a chat board for fellow daters with more useful tips including setting prices and warning signs of a bad potential date. Once it was late enough, she went by a convenience store to pick up some stuff for breakfast, retrieved her stuff from the train station, then headed to the love hotel she'd found in the area. It had fully automated room check in, enabling her to avoid dealing with the issue of her age, and the lower cost rooms were less garish and lacking the odd-ball themes that the more expensive ones had. As long as it had a huge tub to soak in and the bed was comfortable that was enough for her.

Out of the tub, she turned on the television to watch a bit of late-night anime while mulling over her day. Before she could stop herself, she found herself reaching for the phone and hitting Akihito's number. But it just came up blocked again. She tried to will herself not to cry, as she'd managed to the night before, but this time the tears would not be denied. She cried long and hard, her sobs wracking her slim body until her eyes ran dry. Even then, she lay huddled on the bed, curled up in a ball until the alarm went off, reminding her she had to check out of the hotel.

Fortunately, the hotel bathroom had supplies she could use to clear up the puffiness in her eyes. "That was it, no more tears over him, them, or any of the rest. We will do what we have to do," she told herself as she looked in the mirror and finished getting ready. It was another day and she had things to do. She needed a safe place to store her things and her money. Eventually the lockers wouldn't be enough, especially if she continued to buy things.

And while the hotels were nice, they would likely get tiresome after a while. One thing that had been consistent in every manga series she had read of teenagers on their own was having their own places to stay. She was two months shy of sixteen, and while she could forge a letter from her parents acting as a guarantor, if the potential landlord tried to call that would result in trouble, maybe even the cops getting involved. That could make getting even a cheap apartment difficult. A hostel was an idea, but hotels at least offered more privacy and she could continue having her own room.

While heading out to find breakfast, she grabbed an apartment magazine to see what the prices were. It wouldn't hurt to at least look at them and see if she couldn't try to get one. She made a list of potentials in her notebook and then started researching what was needed to rent an apartment.

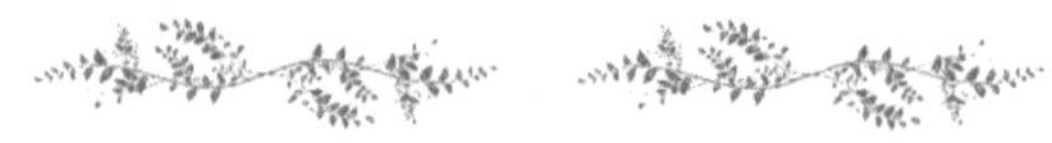

HER APARTMENT HUNTING WAS a bust. Every place she tried refused her if she didn't have a parent as a guarantor, well except for one place where the owner had offered to let her stay, in exchange for free services whenever he wanted. She was glad they had met outside, and she got away from him as fast as she could. Fortunately, the love hotel she was staying in was clean and well run, most nights she even could get the same room. It wasn't "home", but it offered some stability.

During the day, she would go to manga cafes and libraries to read and continue researching, her evenings on dates. Some days when she had an extra late night or just wanted some quiet, she'd pay for day use of the hotel room, but she tried not to do it too often since it cost another 5,000 yen. While she could afford it with the money she earned from dates, she had learned from her dumping to be frugal about her spending so she would never be caught unawares again.

Her initial dates were all platonic, mostly older men looking to recapture a little youth by hanging out with cute, younger girls for a while. She did a group date with some men in their 30s and 40s with three other girls from the boards. It was fun to get to meet some other girls in the trade and talk with them a bit. They'd exchanged info so they could keep in touch, though it was mostly by message since they were all high schoolers who were just wanting money to spoil themselves. None of them were trying to earn a living like Yuna was. Still, they were nice, as were the guys, and she walked away with 15,000 yen just to be sweet and flattering to some lonely office workers.

Another date involved a 54-year-old man who wanted a companion for dinner and a movie. He was nice, if a bit shy, and had tipped her generously after. While talking, he said he tended to go with enjo kōsai because high school girls were more honest and straight forward, which he felt made the conversations more interesting and the time spent with them livelier. He always felt he had learned something from his dates and left with lots of new things to think about.

Many of her dates were like that, middle-aged or older men, just wanting someone to talk to, or to listen to them, and give them a little attention. They were mostly lonely and too busy with work to even consider trying the dating scene. Some even were intimidated by women in their dating age range, so they went for "professionals" who could make them feel at ease and just let them have fun without all the pressures of dating with marriage in mind.

While still looking for a safe place to truly call home, she continued storing her belongings at the train locker, including her extra cash. She stowed a little emergency money in the lining of the pocket of her jacket, which she'd carefully ripped then stitched back closed with a small sewing kit she'd purchased. Still, she grew increasingly concerned about her long-term prospects, as there was a limit to how much she could store in the locker.

A week after their first day, Hoji called to check on her. He seemed sad and angry at her parents for never coming to get her, but also somewhat relieved as it meant he didn't have to try another new girl. He arranged to be her date for the evening, offering her 50,000 yen. She'd been glad to see him call, as she really had enjoyed her first date with him, and it was nice to be able to talk to someone more openly about her situation, even if he only knew part of the truth. He was also one of the few hot guys she'd dated so far, and she wasn't about to object to that. The money, of course, was a bonus, particularly with his generous over-paying. This time he'd asked if she could dress up a bit and took her to the restaurant at the top of the hotel where he'd gotten her a room before.

"So, Yuna-chan, how are you coming along?" he asked while swirling his wine in his glass.

"Okay, I guess. I mean, nothing bad has happened yet, other than not being able to go home. I tried calling, but they hung up on me. When I tried again later, they'd changed their phone number."

He frowned. "That really is a shame. It's hard to believe parents could be so cruel like that. Where are you staying? Are you getting enough to eat?"

She nodded. "Mostly in rooms at a love motel not far from here. It's clean and I can usually get the same room, which is kind of nice. I tried to find an apartment, but no one will rent to someone my age except one pervy guy who wanted extra 'favors' in exchange. He scared me a little, but I was able to get away."

"Thank goodness. You need to be careful. There are some people who will try to take advantage of you, especially if they learn about your current situation," he said it in a more matter-of-fact tone than a lecturing one, which she'd appreciated.   He stroked his chin thoughtfully before continuing. "You know, I have an old friend who might be able to help you. You seem like a sweet girl, so I think she'd be okay with it. You actually remind me of her a little. She's a former classmate of mine and runs a set of boarding rooms not too far away. With me giving you a reference, she might overlook your age and rent to you. It's a basic room, but should be affordable and it would certainly be safer. If that's okay with you, I mean?"

"Wow, really? That would be awesome! If you really think she'd go for it?"

"I'm sure she will. I'll give her a call tomorrow and let you know."

True to his word, the next afternoon around two, Hoji called and directed her to meet his friend in an hour. It required Yuna to take the train, but it was only a stop away so it was convenient to the area she was familiar with. Hoji's friend turned out to be an attractive young woman with her blue and green hair cut into a long buzz cut, piercings in her ears, and wearing a short skirt and a halter top. Yuna couldn't help staring, not able to picture a calm, business man like Hoji being friends with someone like her. As if she could read her mind, the woman laughed.

"I know, I know, it doesn't look like that stick in the mud and I would be friends, but we've known each other for ages. Don't let him fool you, he used to have a wild streak too. Anyway, pleased to meet you Yuna-chan. I'm Chika. Hoji said you have a bit of a situation, so he's acting as your guardian and guarantor for the place, which is fine with me. His word is gold, you can count on that."

If Hoji was calming, Chika was like a wild wind, impossible to pin down. But Yuna loved her easy-going nature and let herself be swept along as Chika led the way to the apartment.

"Here you go. It's not huge or anything, but it's clean, safe, and all yours if you want it. Everything you see is included. You'll need your own futon and fridge and probably want to get dishes and cookware."

The apartment was a 16-jō studio style unit, with a basic, functional kitchen on one side with a tiled floor, a single counter and a two-burner cooktop. There was enough space for her to have a small microwave and an apartment-sized fridge. The rest was a combination living, dining, and bedroom area with tatami mats on the floors. There was a wall A/C for the summer and a newer looking kerosene heater for the winter. A door off the room led to a combination toilet room and bathroom, which, much to Yuna's delight, included an actual bathtub with the shower. It even had a small washer included and a balcony off the living area where she could hang her clothes out to dry. Sliding panels revealed that the walls by the doors to the bathroom contained storage space, with room for her clothes and a place to store her futon. It wasn't huge, but it was bigger than some she'd seen. It was certainly enough space for just her.

"It's perfect. I'd love to stay here. How much do I owe for the deposit?"

"Don't worry about it, Hoji said he'd act as your guarantor and that he'll cover the deposit and key money. Rent is 75,000 yen a month, payable on the first and I'll prorate this month for you. Water and electricity are included in that, but gas and Internet, if you want it, is separate. Since you mostly work at night, that should be fine. A lot of people here do too, so you'll find it pretty quiet in the morning."

"Did Hoji tell you what I do?" Yuna asked.

Chika nodded. "Yeah, but it doesn't bother me. To be honest, I did the same thing when I was your age."

"Seriously? Just for fun or…"

"Nope, I was a little older than you, but I was on my own after my parents died and it was a way to make ends meet. I'm probably too old to give you many good tips, but one that doesn't age with time is make sure you never bring any clients here for your own safety, okay? And always watch for being followed, some guys can be real creeps."

Yuna nodded. She had never told any of them, except Hoji, which love motel she stayed at either. That had been one of the first tips she'd seen on the boards and one repeated a lot. Never let them know where you live, not even the general area, just in case you picked up any crazies.

"If you need anything, my place is apartment one, on the bottom floor in the corner. I'm usually up late and I like to sleep in, though if there is an emergency don't hesitate to wake me up. There is a drop box outside my door for dropping in your rent if I'm not home. Just put it in an envelope with your name and apartment number on it." Chika held out the keys for Yuna. "There ya go. If you want to grab your stuff and move in now that would be fine. Oh, and there is a great consignment shop around the corner that you might want to pop in to pick up dishes and stuff. Tell them you're living here and Dajh will give you a discount."

"Oh, great, thank you. Thank you so much," Yuna said, bowing deeply. She rode the train back to the station to empty out her locker and carried her things to the apartment. She'd managed to save up just over 100,000 yen from her week's earnings, which she stuffed in her purse. As Chika had promised, the store nearby had almost everything she needed, and she was able to get dishes, some basic cookware, a rice cooker, a kotatsu, and a few odds and ends for 30,000 yen, after the discount. Chika's friend also directed her to a place not far away where she could get a new futon and some bedding, which combined with a fridge and microwave took a good chunk of the remaining funds.

By the time she got groceries, she was short on cash, but she wasn't too worried. She'd make more tonight, and thanks to not having to do a deposit, she had all month to build up enough to cover the rent and utilities. Everything was put away just in time to get out to work.

That night, to help replenish her dwindling funds, she took on a client that wanted sex. The client was a 66-year-old man who wanted a blow job. It was hard to get started with his wrinkled skin and aged smell, but she used the thought of the 40,000 yen payment, in advance, to perform enthusiastically enough to make him happy.

After she left his hotel room, she ducked into an alley and puked up the salty load he'd had her swallow along with what was left of her lunch. That had been harder than she'd thought, and she resolved herself not to take on anymore sex clients unless they were young and good looking enough for her to enjoy it some too. Still, it was enough money that she didn't bother doing a second date and headed back to her new home to finish unpacking and getting settled in.

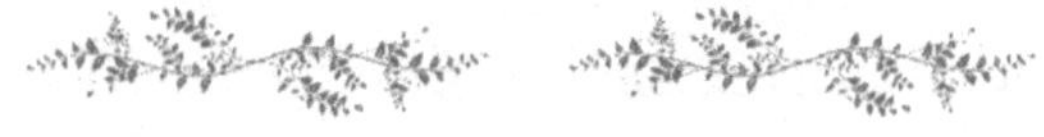

CHIKA TURNED OUT TO be a great landlord and fun to talk to when they were both free, even though she was almost Hoji's age. Yuna appreciated having an actual friend for the first time, though it was also hard for her to know how to act or what was right or wrong to say, so in some ways she acted with Chika just as she did with clients, at least behaviorally. Unlike with them, she didn't feel the need to lie a lot to Chika, though she hadn't told her the full truth about her past, any more than she had Hoji. One thing she had figured out by this point was that telling anyone about Akihito would not go over well.

Yuna had begun interacting more with other girls in the area who were engaged in the same field as her. Most of them were much different from she was, though, with many being overall good girls from nice families who mostly did dates on the weekends to earn money for and get gifts of expensive brand name clothing items and accessories. During the week they went to high school and often did club activities. Two girls she met were even in their school's student council! For them it was just something to do for fun, to enjoy the attention and the perks. They tended to avoid any clients looking for sex and most also ignored requests from foreigners because of the language barrier and a fear of how they might act. Still, they were great sources for learning how to talk and act more like a girl her age, which several clients enjoyed.

Even after moving into the new place, Yuna continued her established routine of using the day time to read, relax, and study on how to be a teenager. It was kind of hilarious that despite now being sixteen herself, she only knew how to be one from reading and applying a lot of manga, light novels, and spending afternoons hanging around areas where other teen girls congregated, like pastry shops and coffee bars. She did it not for company, though, but to study, to learn. Somewhere along the way, she'd decided she was going to be the best damned date anyone could ask for, and learning how became a sort of school she created for herself.

She picked up a video game system just to learn about games for the clients that were into geekier girls. As her income grew and she'd built up a decent amount of savings, she decided to get a laptop computer to help with records. After using borrowed library books to brush on how to use it and learn more specialized programs, she could track all her client records. She even made a database of them, not for potential blackmail or anything shady like that, but with notes and the like. It made it even easier to be perfect for her regulars, as she always "remembered" their likes, dislikes, and little things they had told her, even if they'd last met two months ago!

Having the laptop also enabled her to better track her finances and to access even more information through the Internet. With Chika's help, she opened a new bank account, enabling her to store her money safely and start earning interest on her savings. Hoji helped her open a brokerage account so that she could start investing in stocks as well.

She'd also used some on-line courses and CD courses to improve her English enough to be able to take on some foreign clients, though she screened those more carefully. They were often much more interesting, because of the cultural differences, but those same differences meant they didn't always know the rules of the dating game. From one nice man from New York, she'd learned about the American version of prostitution and how those women were treated. It was scary sounding and made her a bit sad that the women there sounded exploited rather than being in charge of their work. Still, they also tended to pay better because many girls would refuse to go on dates with them at all, due to the language barrier.

Yuna now regularly took on clients wanting sex, though she mostly limited to once a week on Friday's as the pay was good enough that she could then take the weekend off, other than when Hoji called for a date, which was usually on Saturday evenings. She also avoided the men looking for anything kinky, sticking to oral sex, hand jobs, and regular sex. Anything mentioning sex toys, S&M, or other fetishes she rejected, along with anal, having no desire to do it again after the one time Akihito had tried it on her. It was the one time he'd physically hurt her during their relationship, and he'd spent weeks spoiling her to make up for it.

Six months after she'd arrived, Hoji planned a special night for them to celebrate her "anniversary". He had a long gown made of a rich purple silk delivered to her apartment, along with a dozen flowers and a request that she wear it on a date with him tonight. Unlike the other dates they'd had to that point, where they just met wherever he'd picked for dinner, this evening he picked her up in his black Mercedes-Benz. It was a sexy car built for speed and Yuna wondered if he ever drove it full speed anywhere.

Dinner was at a chic, expensive restaurant with a menu full of foods and words she didn't know. Still, it was fun and he treated her like a princess. While they waited for dessert, he gave her a gorgeous gold chain with a pendant of a pine tree hanging from it, calling it a symbol of her tenacity. After dinner, he'd asked her if she would be willing to go back to his apartment with him. Though they hadn't negotiated any additional rate, Yuna didn't hesitate at all when he kissed her. With the way he'd spoiled her already, how much help he'd given her in getting established, and the true attraction for him she'd developed over the months, she didn't mind adding it to the date at all.

After that, Hoji became one of her regular sex clients as well, upping his pay from his already generous amount to an astounding 90,000 yen per date! Even with sex, her other clients usually just paid 40-50,000 yen. When he'd given her the first increased amount, she'd looked at him in surprise and asked if he was sure that's how much he intended to give. He'd laughed and said yes, because she made him so happy when he was with her and because he looked forward to seeing what kind of future she would make for herself with the right support.

Though she was enjoying herself now, Yuna was already well aware that she wasn't working in anything that could be a lifelong career. An enjo kōsai girl was not like being a professional geisha or something. She knew once she reached her twenties, at best, she would be too old to find good clients. Both with requests she accepted and those she didn't, the preference was for teenage girls or really pretty, young looking women. While Yuna followed a strict beauty regimen to help her maintain and optimize her cuteness, she couldn't count on it lasting forever. Her mom had been an adorable girl in high school, but a plain, ordinary looking one as an adult.

Though she wasn't sure yet what she wanted to do in the future, she had long since figured out that having just a middle school education would severely limit her options and mostly resign her to working as a store clerk for the rest of her life. After living the life she was used to with the pay from her current job, the idea of going down to something so cheap was just not worth considering. At Chika's encouragement, she added to her "day school" by signing up for a real one. It let her work towards earning her high school degree without having to attend regular high school and was done mostly through correspondence and online courses. And unlike a regular high school, she could enroll without her parents' permission. It was almost fun learning again, as it filled up her otherwise relatively dull days with something to do.

Hoji had asked if she'd considered going on to university, but without knowing what she wanted to do, it seemed kind of pointless. She tried some of those "what's the best career for you" type quizzes in magazines, but nothing they came up with sounded interesting. Sales? Well, she was good at selling herself, but what else could she sell that anyone would want to buy and that she could sell with as much enthusiasm and authenticity? Secretarial work sounded boring, and with her past, things like medicine and legal careers were not even options. Teaching?

Hoji thought she would be good at modeling or acting, but the media would rip her apart as soon as they learned about her past, and it was doubtful she'd be able to get any good roles. Even in the porn industry, she'd read directors wanted more stars with good academic backgrounds and that there were so many amateurs trying to enter the industry, she'd be unlikely to make the cut for more than one or two videos. It would be no different from the dating, except she'd be even less certain of making a daily income.

Despite having no plans for the long-term future, Yuna was mostly happy and enjoying her life. It wasn't an ordinary life, to be sure, and while others might have looked down at her for her profession, she was living the way she chose. She regularly had clients who not only spoiled her with presents but also took her on trips, including one to Hong Kong for a whole week! She visited Tokyo Disneyland multiple times, along with other theme parks, visited art museums, went to concerts, and all sorts of fun activities. And there were no parents to try to dictate what she should do, no Akihito controlling who she talked to and trying to own her, and no boss controlling her salary. She viewed herself as an entrepreneur and business woman.

Present

"ADACHI?" YUNA'S CALLING MY name woke me from the silence I'd fallen into after she'd long since stopped talking.

"Sorry, I'm just in awe," I told her honestly. At her age, she truly had taken the lemons of life and made lemonade, best-selling, award-winning level lemonade. And she'd been damned smart about it, well beyond her years. I know I should have been disgusted she'd been a prostitute and did compensated dating, but she made it sound like it was just as much a job as anything else. "Truly, I can't help admiring how you went about turning your life around."

It was perhaps the first time I'd seen her blush or look anything remotely close to shy or embarrassed. "I just did what seemed right. Being well-read helped a lot and being able to learn from some of my senpai. Their posts on the board really helped me spot the mistakes new girls make, as well as how to adjust what they usually did for the sake of earning a living."

"If I may I ask, did you like it?"

"Hmmm, on the whole, I did. I really did. The dates were usually fun. I met a lot of interesting people and got to learn about some different cultures. I had a few clients who took me on trips to Hong Kong, Okinawa, Taiwan, even London once. I loved being able to set my own hours and decide who I would and wouldn't see. And I really can't complain about the pay at all, it was better than any 'normal' job I could have gotten." She paused, head tilted slightly to the side. "I don't want to give the impression it was all roses and sunshine. I mean I don't regret the choice myself, and I don't think it's anything to be ashamed of. It was a job. I sold only what I had to sell, myself and my time. I really don't get why people act all uptight about it, it doesn't hurt anyone, it's just giving people your time."

I knew she had a point, but I felt I needed to play devil's advocate for the sake of being complete. "What about married clients or those otherwise in relationships? Would you say it still doesn't hurt anyone?"

She gave me an almost approving look. "That is true, in that case the guy could be hurting his significant other, but it also is more nuanced I think. If he spends two hours being flattered by me and goes home happier, treating his wife better than he has in ages, and feeling virile and manly, did it hurt her or did it benefit her as well? It is true, some use us to cheat on their partners, but for me that is between them. I'm just providing the service, I'm not responsible for it being used to hurt others, any more than someone who sells swords is responsible for someone buying one and then accidentally cutting up their arm because they have no idea how to use one. It comes down to personal responsibility there. I suppose I should note though that I didn't go out of my way to find married clients, I just never asked either. It wasn't my business, in my opinion."

It was an interesting response, and one that felt closer to my own than I would have expected. I never understood why people blamed the "other person" when there was cheating in the relationship. Was it not their actual partner who made the choice and did the cheating? The other person hadn't made the commitment or agreed to be monogamous or any of that. Was it so much easier to put the anger on the unknown target than admit your choice of partner ended up being a possible mistake?

Yuna yawned and began making ready to go to sleep. With a small smile, I put away my notebook then joined her in the bed. It wasn't a perfect bed by any stretch, but that night it felt like heaven lying there with Yuna wrapped in my arms as we drifted off to sleep.

The Fifth Day

Present

I WOKE IN A COLD sweat, jerking upright even before I fully realized I was awake. Once again my nightmares had been filled with the Nakamura's, only this time their ghosts chased me around an abstract version of Hakodate. The children clung to my arms with ephemeral bodies that still had tiny organs and veins visible, blood-stained vomit flowing down their semi-translucent clothes. Over and over, as they phased in and out of visibility, they asked me why, why I'd killed them. Mrs. Nakamura floated nearby, her appearance similar with a plaintive look on her face as she wailed and wailed until my ears ached.

Warm arms wrapped around me. "It's okay, you're safe now. It's okay." Yuna's soft, calm voice flowed through me, chasing the remnants of the dreams away. I wanted to cry, but I couldn't bring myself to let go in front of her like that, at least not that morning.

Instead I gave my head a little shake and patted her hand. "Thank you. Sorry about that, just a bad dream. Mind if I go to the bathroom?"

"Sure, go ahead. I'll wait here. Come back soon, it's chilly."

"Will do." I kissed her forehead before slipping out of bed, dressing quickly, then going outside, flashlight in hand to help me find the communal toilet. Tempting as it was to give in to the shaking inside, I pushed myself to get done and back within five minutes. She'd let me go by myself in a public place, I wasn't about to abuse that trust by lingering for no reason.

When I returned and crawled back into bed, she kissed my chin as she slid her body against mine. Desperate to chase the last vestiges of the nightmare away, I claimed her mouth in a silent request. She answered in kind, her warm body and sweet touches giving me the relief I needed at last. After we were sated, we fell back asleep, a nice dreamless sleep that left me more refreshed than the night's version had.

It was mid-morning before we finally roused ourselves enough to enjoy a warm breakfast with some fresh fruit from the camp ground's store. When we were done, we had to keep our showers short to have enough time to get packed and cleaned up before check out time. We could have afforded a second night, but Yuna hadn't seemed inclined to stay there for the rest of our time together.

Instead, we headed out back around the lake, going the other way from the way we came in. It took several hours, as she randomly stopped and stared over the water with a peaceful look on her face. As the morning passed though, rather than enjoying the serenity of the lake, I grew increasingly uneasy. She'd never let us go this far into the day without prompting me for my part of the story, and yet so far there had been no opening question, just smiles and talking only as needed.

Finally, as we finished circling the lake and reentered the woods, I broached the subject. "Yuna, you haven't asked your question for today."

"I know." She looked back at me with a smile that seemed almost sad. "I have two left and they kind of go together. It only seems right to ask them on our next-to-last morning together instead of today. Did you not enjoy this morning's break?"

"Oh, no, I did. You know I did." I smiled at her as an image of our love making slipped through our minds. But the smile fell away almost before it finished forming. If she had two left, one would surely be why I was there. But what could the other be, and why did they need to be together? The only thing I could guess would be why I had been so determined to stop her. That at least would fit with what I knew she knew about me unless she really had recognized me that first time we met and just hadn't said anything.

The rest of the day was spent mostly in companionable silence. I spent much of it thinking over the Nakamura incident, trying to think of how I would tell the story efficiently, tempted to look for ways to avoid telling her too much but knowing I couldn't avoid it. All pre-planning would get me would hopefully being able to tell it without breaking down.

That day was also the day we walked the longest distance we had yet. Circling the lake had to have been a good
8 or 9 kilometers alone, but Yuna did not seem satisfied
until we were back on the east side of the woods. By the
time we did stop, I was half tempted to just shout the story
at her just to get it out and over with, but that would break
the deal. The night time was hers and there was still a lot
of story left between her being a sixteen-year-old entrepreneur and a twenty-two-year-old suicidal woman.

Life Goes On

WHILE YUNA WAS EXTREMELY careful with her dates, she did have a few bad ones. One client who'd requested a normal sex date turned out to be rough and violent. He left her face bruised to the point she was forced to spend a week away from dating while it healed enough for make-up to conceal it. While the man had still paid the original agreed-to cost of 50,000 yen, he hadn't been inclined to tip extra for the damage he did or to help with any medical costs. Chika helped her treat the wounds and Yuna made sure to post a warning about him on the boards for other girls like her, to hopefully keep him from getting anyone else.

She was picked up by the cops twice in her first year of

being active. The first had let her go with a fatherly warning after she'd cried and acted like it was her first time and told him her "sad story" of being ordered to do it by her boyfriend to show she loved him. Fortunately, it had been outside of her regular territory so she hadn't run into him again.

The second hadn't been interested in pleas. He worked the beat in her area and had seen her enough to know she was bullshitting anyway. Instead, they'd come to a deal where he'd keep her from being hassled and he could come to her regularly for free quickies and blow jobs in secluded spots he knew about. Yuna never really saw it as blackmail and considered him a favorite regular, even if he didn't pay her himself. He did send clients her way, particularly foreigners, and after she met him, she had someone she could go to if a client got rough. He would handle things off the record for her. He even gave her gifts now and then, nothing too expensive on his salary, but small trinkets and a stuffed cop bear that she thought looked like him.

And so, her time passed, and she moved from sixteen to seventeen, still living in the same small apartment, still seeing five to six clients a week, sometimes more, and her dates with Hoji almost always came the first Saturday of the month. It was his extravagant payments that enabled her to cut back on how many dates she did a week, plus continuing to do at least one sex date a week. Any unpleasantness over the past two years had been to her nothing more than mere blips in her otherwise unfettered life. Easily put aside for the comfort of a well-funded life.

Unlike many of her cohorts, who often only worked a few months unless they were working with pimps, Yuna's necessity of paying her own way made her almost obsessively frugal. While she spent money on outfits, including new school uniforms and other cute clothes for dates, she didn't live excessively, mostly cooked at home when not being fed by dates, and saved relentlessly. It was the one thing she was certain of about the future: She didn't ever want to be caught as she'd been when she'd been abandoned, penniless and forced to act out of dire need.

At seventeen, she'd amassed a healthy savings of over 10 million yen, more than enough to cover a long gap when she was ready to quit. Not that she intended to early, she aimed to continue working until she was at least 21. It was still young enough to keep most clients happy and for her to still be enjoying what she did. By then she'd have significantly more money, more options, and maybe even an idea of what she wanted to do next.

Every day, for the first year after she'd been left, Yuna continued making the trip to the spot where she'd been left, hoping against hope that Akihito would still come for her. He'd never unblocked her number, though, and on the one-year anniversary of the start of her new life, she'd stood in that spot and finally whispered goodbye to him and the past that had long since forgotten her.

In doing so, she'd been able to let go of the last of her lingering feelings for her brother, while also accepting that he'd never truly loved her and that she was better off without him. She'd also given up on her parents, forcing herself to consider them dead to her, along with the rest of her family. From that day forward, she presented herself as an orphan to anyone other than Chika and Hoji, who already knew she'd been abandoned.

Then, one chilly fall afternoon, she had an unexpected

shock. She'd gone to meet a client, a young man of about twenty-two looking for conversation and sex. He was barely paying the minimum and hadn't posted a picture, but his profile indicated he was a regular with the service posting his ad and he had a good reputation. In the mood for an easy job, she went ahead and claimed it, then made her way to the indicated love hotel where he was waiting.

Nothing could have prepared her for what she saw when the door opened. Older, his hair longer and more unkempt and with a cigarette dangling from his lips stood Noritaka. She stood in mute silence for a moment until he'd asked her if something was wrong. Considering her brother's beating of him, it probably wasn't the wisest thing to do, but on trembling legs she entered the room and let him close the door behind her. She stopped there, just inside the entrance as he walked around her.

"You're really cute," he finally said after he stopped in front of her, giving her that all too familiar grin. It faltered a bit as he looked at her longer, his head cocked to one side. "It probably sounds like some cheesy pick up line, but you seem kinda familiar."

For a moment, she debated playing it off and getting on with the date, but something in her wanted him to see her, to acknowledge her. "Don't you recognize me Noritaka-kun?"

"I…" He leaned in and looked at her more closely, then jumped back away from her, his eyes wide. "Yuna!? No way, you can't be Yuna…can you?"

She nodded and took a step forward, but he backed away again so she stopped, her hands clutched in front of her chest. "I don't really know what to say to you, not after all this time. If I'd known it was you, I probably wouldn't have come. I mean, Akihito hurt you so bad because of me. I don't blame you if you hate me."

"No! No! I mean, I don't hate you. You were a kid, and I was kind of screwed up in the head. He had every right to kick my ass." Recomposing himself somewhat, he took a few steps forward. "I don't hate you, I swear. I'm just so surprised. I mean…you, you are the girl I hired, right?"

"Yep, I am," she replied, oddly relieved.

"Wow. Okay, now I'm really all messed up. Here, um, let's sit down or something. Sorry, I didn't think to get a room with chairs." He sat on the edge of the bed and patted the spot beside him. "But come on, I can't believe you're…I gotta know how this happened, how you ended up here?"

Yuna plopped down beside him and for the first time in years told the truth, the truth about what happened between her and Akihito, their parents dumping her, and how she'd wound up there. When she was done, they sat in silence a few minutes, Noritaka seemingly stunned by her story.

"Man…that sick…I'm sorry. When he attacked me that day, he was saying stuff like you were his and no one else was allowed to have you, stuff like that. I thought it was off, but he was being so crazy violent at the time, I didn't really stop to think it through. I mean, I always figured if he found out he'd punch me or something, but I think he really was trying to kill me. At the hospital, I ended up telling my parents the truth, or at least part of it, about me kissing you and stuff, but I didn't tell them what he'd said. Maybe if I had…" he shook his head. "Anyway, as soon as I was released, my parents decided to move because they were afraid he'd come after me again. I ended up in Sendai where my grandparents live. Then I moved down here to Tokyo for college and ended up staying."

"What do you do now?" she asked.

"I managed to get an offer at a pretty decent sized company. Right now, I'm in their public relations department, learning the ropes. It's one of those places that just grabs a ton of students just before they graduate, to train up lifetime employees, but I'm not sure if that's really for me. I've been thinking about trying for one of the international firms, where you can apply for something you are interested in, not just getting shifted around all the time. I mean, I studied accounting, because that's what I enjoy."

She nodded. Several clients in their twenties vented about the rigors of the shoshoku katsudo system, how stifling it was, and wondering why they even bothered studying specific subjects in school. It wasn't something she could really understand either, and it sounded like a miserable sort of way to spend the rest of your life, but others seemed happy with it. Hoji, for example, had spoken fondly of his experiences in working in different departments and that he looked forward to learning more as he moved around.

"I'm glad you're doing okay now. I'm really sorry again about my brother." Yuna stood to leave. "I should probably get going."

"Going?"

"Well, I mean, you probably don't want to have a date with me?"

"No, please stay." He reached out and took her hand. "I mean, I don't mind it being you at all. I'm so happy to get to see you again. I've never forgotten you, not ever. I swear." He gently pulled her back to stand in front of him, then leaned his head against her stomach. "I always loved you, that much was true. I thought you'd be my wife, that we'd always be together, then I messed it all up. I shouldn't have touched you back then, even if that was what we'd have in the future, I should have waited until you were older, until we were older. I…"

She wrapped her arms around his head, gently stroking his hair. "It's okay, Noritaka, it really is okay. I know now that it was wrong, at least as far as our ages went, but it's hard to really be mad or anything because you never hurt me, I promise. You were always so sweet and gentle with me. And I loved you too, so much. I thought we'd have a happy life together, that you, me, and Akihito, that we would always be together, just like back then."

Noritaka eased himself back, then reached up to stroke her cheek. "Yuna, can I kiss you, just one more time?"

She leaned in and pressed her lips to his, letting it linger as long as he wanted. At some point he'd pulled her into his lap, just as when she'd been a child and him a not-yet-grown teen. Only now she returned his kiss as an equal, her arms around his neck as she shifted her body enticingly, encouraging him to take the one thing he'd never been able to have with her before.

Soon enough they were lying in the bed, Noritaka on top of her, inside her, moving as if she was a glass figurine that might break at any moment while his hands touched her face, her neck, anywhere he could touch. Just as the Noritaka of her memories had so many times, he'd whispered of his love, of his longing, but now the whispers were tinged with regrets and his eyes filled with tears.

After it was over, they lay together, his arms wrapped

tight around her to hold her there, still randomly peppering her faces with kisses. "You want to leave here? Go somewhere else? We could start over, start the life we dreamed of?"

"What about her?" she asked as she lightly ran a finger over the wedding band decorating his hand.

"Suzaki? I swear, I don't love her, I never did. My parents pressured me into marrying early, afraid that what had happened with you meant I had some kind of twisted thing for children. No matter how much I explained to them, they didn't understand that it had nothing to do with that, that it was just because it was you, my first love, my only love." He kissed her again. "Suzaki is just the daughter of one of my dad's business associates, he came up with the pairing. Apparently she had some kinda trouble in high school too and got chased off, though she is such a bitch I'm not surprised. Either way, I don't like her, hell I can't even stand touching her. That's why I hire dates sometimes. I sure as heck don't want to have sex with her. She isn't you. I know it's not perfect, but you and me can finally be together like we should have, right?"

Yuna shook her head, pity running through her as she realized just how sad and miserable Noritaka had become. She stood and began dressing. "Even if she is awful, it would make me no better to take you from her. For better or worse, I'm sure she depends on you to help support her. Besides, we couldn't be happy together now. We're very different people and you can't return to the past. I'm not that little girl anymore, blindly in love with you and who would be happy just to be with you. I'm my own woman and used to being on my own. You aren't the Noritaka of back then either. Our lives have gone down different paths now."

He wrapped his arms around his knees, despair evident in every line of his body even as he made no move to stop her.

"But, Noritaka, I'm glad we got to meet again. I'm glad we got to have the closure we'd been denied before." She walked back to the bed and kissed the top of his head. "Please, go home and be happy now. I need to know you'll be happy, okay?"

Yuna walked out of the room, his voice calling her name, begging her to stay just a little longer, echoing through her mind. When she got home, she collapsed on the bed in a puddle of tears, crying for the boy who'd not become the man she'd imagined, the little girl who'd never had a chance to really be a child, and the woman who'd realized that even as she'd said those seemingly kind words to Noritaka, it had only been Yuna the actress who tried to say exactly what her clients needed and wanted to hear.

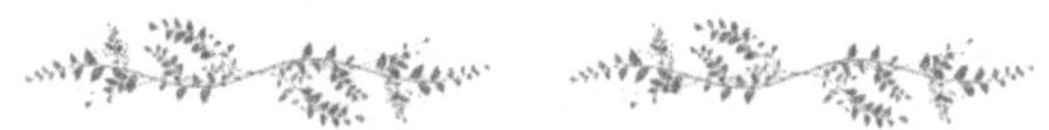

A FEW WEEKS AFTER her date with Noritaka, Yuna had another shock of a much more distressing kind. Namely her period was a month late and showed no signs of coming. Two drug store tests later confirmed she was pregnant. Part of her wondered if it was Noritaka's, though it could have been any of several clients, depending on how far along she was. She had no desire for a child, of course, but clients didn't like having to pull out, and while she always carried condoms, few were willing to use them.

It wasn't the first time someone in her trade got pregnant, though, and a quick trip to the boards got her the name of a trusted doctor who could abort the pregnancy for her while maintaining her confidentiality. The procedure just took a few hours. She had some bleeding and cramping after, but the doctor gave her some pain medication to help with it, and had her use a heating pad. Though it cost her 150,000 yen, she ended up having to stay away from dating for most of a week before she felt up to trying to do any dates. Even then it was another two before she could take on sex dates again.

The same doctor who did the abortion prescribed her pills to help keep her from getting pregnant. She was hesitant about them, as they sounded like an unnatural thing to have in her body, but he'd assured her they were safe and that they were the best way to avoid pregnancy in the future. As long as she took them properly and followed the instruction pamphlet he'd given her, she was almost guaranteed not to get pregnant, even with clients who wouldn't use condoms. While she'd seen some scary stories about side effects on the boards, she decided it was better than having another pregnancy.

She wasn't sure what her future held long term, but she knew right now a baby was not any part of the picture.

Present

 I'd expected I would hear about in that day's session, learning that Yuna had been reunited with Noritaka had not been amongst them. When she'd first said he'd been in that room, I'd almost stopped writing from the shock. That they'd had that kind of visit surprised me more. Though I guess by now, I shouldn't be surprised. In the five days we'd been together, I'd realized that Yuna seemed to hold no blame or anger over her brother or Noritaka's misdeeds at all, so that she had forgiven him, and even continued the "date" with him, shouldn't have shocked me.

But part of me was still bothered by it, that he'd come back into her life at all, much less as a married man while still saying he loved her. It seemed unfair to me, cruel and unfair to both Yuna and the wife who was waiting for him somewhere while he had his date with Yuna. Of course, I knew many clients of girls engaged in enjo kōsai, even for sex dates, were married. And the point of the dates was not some romantic liaison, but just a bit of distraction from the everyday boringness that was life.

The silence between us stretched on, as my mind focused on the fact that she'd gotten pregnant before, much less had an abortion. I was in no place to judge her for that. While she made good money from her dating time that would have all come crashing down if she'd had a child to watch over, and at only seventeen she was much too young to be an unwed mother. Besides, our country was not generally kind to such women, even less than they would be to Yuna over her occupation. She'd have a much harder time finding a new field and likely be shunned from renting in many complexes. My divorced sister had gone through some hellish experiences trying to find a home and raising her son. Being an unwed mother by choice would have been even worse.

Still, I wondered if the decision had been as easy for her as she'd made it sound. "Was it hard for you to do? The abortion I mean?"

"No, not at all. The doctor I went to worked with several other girls from the trade, so they weren't surprised I wanted to terminate. It hurt for a few days, but that was it."

"Ah, no, sorry, I meant making the decision to have it?"

She shook her head with a self-derisive laugh. "Not at all. I wouldn't curse some innocent child to having someone like me for a mother. He or she will be much better off with whoever they go to when they are born. Besides, how could I take care of a baby while working? Sure, I had enough savings to take off for maybe a year or two, but then what? My body would have stretch marks and it would no longer be cute and youthful, which were keys to my being so good at my job. I'd have gotten fatter and it would have been obvious just from the changes pregnancy render on the body that I was a woman. No, it was maybe one of the easiest decisions I'd made. I'm sure the child thanked me too, for not being so selfish as to bring it into such a miserable existence."

"I see." I took a few more notes. "If you don't mind me asking, did it give you closure? Meeting Noritaka again?"

"It did, yes. I think at that point I was finally able to let go of the last vestiges of my past. I cried, sure, but it also felt a bit like I'd been set free, free of chains I didn't even know had been tied around me. After that day, I was able to get myself to delete my parents' and my brother's phone numbers from my address book. I also finally threw away my old house key, which I'd kept in my safe box all that time. I'd realized that it really was as I'd told Noritaka, that the past was the past, it was something behind us that we can never return to. We can only keep walking forward. I stopped looking behind me at the shadows from my past, I stopped letting those ghosts haunt my every move, and just focused on the here and now and the future."

Her words stung home like a hornet's barb. Ever since the thing with the Nakamuras had happened, my time had frozen and I'd gotten stuck replaying the past I couldn't change repeatedly. I'd let myself wallow in self-pity and regret, not seeing what it was doing to me and those around me. It still ached to think about, my mistakes, my regrets, but now, I knew I was ready to tell her, tell this girl who'd shared so much with me already about my own terrible crime.

But that night she'd talked long enough, and besides, that wasn't our pattern. My time would come in the morning. As if she could tell the things going through my mind, Yuna smiled at me and leaned in to brush her lips against mine. "Tomorrow morning. And then, come evening, I'll tell you the last of my story."

"Okay." I put away my notebook and we turned out the light. I worried that the thoughts of the coming conversation would leave me up all night, but instead I fell fast asleep as soon as our love making had concluded, my arms still wrapped around her tight.

The Sixth Day

Present

THE NIGHTMARES THAT NIGHT were the worse yet, and I woke up multiple times during the night filled with fear and regret. Every time, Yuna would comfort me in a low, soothing voice until I fell back asleep, never questioning, simply supporting. Sometime before morning the ghosts of the Nakamuras finally let me sleep in peace, though even that dreamless sleep was fitful and brought little rest.

In the morning, we went through our usual routine, even though I was half asleep. As she had the day before, Yuna let me go off to do my bathroom break myself, but now I was the one anxious to be near her, to the point I beat her back to the tent. Breakfast was a quick, quiet affair. And then the time came. We sat there together, watching each other almost as if waiting for one of us to make the first move. It was Yuna, of course, who broke the silence.

"So, Adachi, who are the Nakamuras and why did you come to this place?"

That she said their name while asking their identity threw me for a loop. "How…?"

"All week you've kept looking at that newspaper article with their name on the headline. It seemed like you looked at it anytime you felt happy or relaxed, so I presumed it was connected."

"Ah, yeah, that makes sense," I replied, then took a deep breath. "Do you remember how I said I wanted to be a truth teller? That it was the reason I became a journalist to begin with? I just wanted to help uncover the truth, the scandals and bad stuff that too often got swept under the rug by the rich and powerful."

She nodded.

"Well, even though I worked in the business and finance, I still fancied myself a future investigative reporter. At one point, I did a story on a new electronics firm that seemed to be doing really well, almost too well for a company its age. My initial story was a fluff piece, something to introduce the company and gush about how great it was. But I thought for sure there had to be something more, something behind their success. So I began doing more digging. My first explorations turned up nothing and seemed to point to it just being a particularly good management staff that had a keen feel for the market and their customer base and a few strokes of good luck that had led to their success."

I looked down at my hands in my lap. "Still, I thought that couldn't be it. No one can be that successful just on that, so I kept digging and digging, so certain there had to be something dirty and corrupt behind it all. Finally, I thought I'd found it, the key to the puzzle. I'd found what seemed to be evidence that the CEO of the company, Nakamura Takuji, had been bribing competitors to over-bid on contracts to enable him to get several key ones quickly. Big conspiracy stuff, you know, like secret meetings between him and a foreign guy who also happened to regularly meet with the CEO of one of his top competitors. Signs of altered documents and, of course what I saw as the biggest sign, their success at winning contracts over older, more established companies.

"I had a few more feelers out to people with more info, including a source who said they could tell me exactly what went on in those meetings. But I was antsy, ready to break the story, so I wrote it up and gave it my editor. He was hesitant, but I was so certain I was right, that on my word that everything had been checked and that it was a solid expose, he agreed to run it."

I paused, still remembering his words, that because I'd always been honest and he saw so much potential in me, that he'd take me at my word. In doing so he'd put the paper and himself at great risk, and at the time I'd been so happy that he'd believed in me so much.

"Then what happened?" she prompted me with an almost pitying look, as if she could see where it was going.

"The story ran. As I held the copy of the paper in my hand, planning how to frame it as my first real story, I got an email from my source. The man Takuji had been meeting was a doctor, a doctor to treat his young son's lymphoma. Though we have good doctors here, Takuji didn't think they could do enough and he was desperate to save him. The doctor was an expert from the United States and had helped the other CEO's sister survive the same illness. What I'd thought were altered documents were just drafts that had been wrongly discarded. Nothing worthy of any real scorn or derision, it happened all the time. Driven by the need to help his son and his own near genius-level business acumen, Takuji had done nothing wrong. He'd just been determined to do all that he could to make his business succeed to afford the expensive treatments and the long trip to America his son would need.

"But the damage had already been done. Multiple partners immediately cut ties with Nakamura. Other papers picked up the story and ran with it, not doing their own checking first. There were calls for Takuji's resignation and for a government investigation. Their stock, barely trading for a year, plummeted to the point it was delisted. I destroyed them, just as I thought I would, but for a mistake, for a false story. Worse, I couldn't bring myself to admit it to my editor, not at first. I hid at home, ignoring the phone calls from him, from other papers wanting to interview me for breaking the story, from the world.

"It was late that night and a few beers later, that I finally managed to get myself to go see Kido, my editor, and blurted out the ugly truth. That the whole thing was wrong, all wrong. I confessed to not waiting for those last few sources to come in, in being too eager to tell the story without being sure the story was right."

"He must have been really hurt when you told him all that," she said quietly.

I nodded. "Yeah. I figured he'd yell at me, curse me, probably fire me, but he just said he was disappointed in me, that he'd thought I'd been ready but clearly he'd been wrong. The look on his face tore through me, worse than if it had been my own father sitting there. I apologized over and over. I think I even cried a bit. Kido, he's a good man, though, a really good man. He said it would take a while to trust me again, that I'd have to start over, but that he'd still stand by me. He'd made the decision to run the story, so he took part of the blame himself. If he hadn't been in the industry so long, he would have probably gotten fired himself, but he was able to hold on and even kept me from getting fired, though I'm still not sure how or why.

"Still, I had to be punished and was put on immediate suspension. A retraction ran the very next day, but Nakamura Industries never recovered. As much press as my story got, the retraction was barely a blip on the radar and just sparingly ran, often buried pages deep. Two weeks after my story ran, Takuji gave up and closed the company. Four hundred employees lost their jobs, knowing that their records were now marred by the stain of that company's name in their job histories."

"And Takuji himself?"

"He and his family sold their home, then disappeared. At first, people presumed they had left the country, taken the boy to America to finish his treatment using whatever savings they had. But then we learned that he had taken every dime he had left in his bank account and split it amongst all those employees, sending them what he could to help them get through until they found another job. Near the start of summer, when the park rangers did one of their regular sweeps for bodies, they found the Nakamura family. Takuji, his wife, their daughter, and that little boy. All dead from having drank poison."

I held my hands out in front of me, the trembling obvious even to my water-filled eyes. "My foolishness, my arrogance had killed them, just as surely as if I'd done the deed myself. They'd felt hopeless, with no way to continue their son's care, so they'd decided they'd all go together and leave the world that had so wronged them. There was a note left behind…a note that said they were sorry they hadn't made things clearer so that there would be no suspicions, apologizing for hurting their workers, and forgiving me for being misinformed and my subsequent misreporting of the situation. Forgave me…how could they forgive me? How?"

At that point, I dissolved into a useless puddle of tears. I half expected her to dismiss me, to scorn me as Hiyori had, but instead I felt Yuna's embrace cover me in warmth and felt her soothing kisses against my hair and brow as she made soft comforting sounds. She let me bawl on and on as I cried out all the self-hatred I'd been holding in the last few months. When the tears finally stopped, I felt strangely calm and serene, as if it had been what I needed to refresh myself, to let myself take that one last step to start walking forward again.

After a bit, she kissed me one more time before pulling back to look at me. "Is that why you came here?"

"Yeah. I…I was able to find out where their bodies were found. I wanted to go to that spot, to…well, to be honest, I'm not sure what. To talk to them, to tell them I'm sorry. It seemed so inadequate compared to what I'd done, but still, something compelled me here. It was the first thing in ages that had gotten me to even leave my apartment."

"Okay then," she said before taking my hands. "Let's

go."

"Go?"

"You wanted to find it, right? So let's go find it. You know where it is right?" she asked as she urged me out of the tent. I nodded and pulled out the map I'd been given. She took a quick look at it then nodded. "You were on your way there when you met me, huh?"

I nodded.

"Sorry."

"It's okay. I don't regret that," I told her with a smile, then leaned down to kiss her lips gently. I think that was the first time I'd initiated a kiss or anything outside of our nights in the tent. She gave me a quick grin, then turned to pull down the tent. Once everything was packed up, she took the lead as usual as we started into the woods.

I knew we were on the east side of the woods again, but I didn't know quite where. Still, she seemed confident as she moved through the trees, her path more sure than usual and with no stopping to look at trees or caves or anything else this time.

At midday, she stopped and checked the map again, then asked if I knew what the exact spot looked like. I nodded and handed her the photograph of the spot, which included markers showing where the bodies had lain. She studied it a moment, then set off again. Less than an hour later, she stopped for a second time then pointed to an area in front of us. "Is this it?"

Holding up the photograph, I compared the two, then checked the description I'd been given along with it. As far as I could tell, this was it; this was the place. I walked forward hesitantly, almost expecting the ghosts from my nightmares to appear for their revenge. Instead it was a quiet little clearing, much like the ones we'd been making our camps in and where I first met her. Yuna hung back, staying near the edge and allowing me to face this task on my own.

At first, there seemed to be no obvious sign that it had been the scene of four deaths, but then I noticed the small arrangement of flowers in the spot where the markers had sat in the photograph. Some other member of the Nakamura family must have come to pay their respects and say goodbye. The sight made me tear up again as I squatted down in front of it. The offering I'd brought had long gone bad and the flowers had wilted in my backpack, so I could only clap my hands together and bow deeply.

Facing that spot, picturing the four of them together, I finally knew what I wanted to say. "Thank you. Thank you for forgiving me. I don't deserve it and I know it. You, more than anyone, have every right to hate me and to have cursed my name with your final words, but instead you extended one final hand of kindness to me. I'm sorry I didn't get to know you better, that I didn't try to know the man behind the story. The man who would give his last dime to his employees and who put others above himself always. I'm sorry I let my foolish pride get in the way of the truth, that I'd forgotten the importance of not letting myself bar myself from seeing what was true and what was false. Most of all, I'm sorry that you paid the price for my sins, that I made you suffer so terribly. I can only hope now you're together somewhere, happy, and that your little boy is healthy and able to run and play again. And I hope that if we meet again, I will have become a much better man, one worthy of the forgiveness that you so graciously extended me."

I bowed again and sent up a silent prayer for them before turning and rejoining Yuna. Tears glistened in her eyes as she hugged me tight. "I'm sure you will be, Adachi. You've already taken the first steps."

I hugged her back, grateful for her words and the sincerity behind them. After we left, she led me through the woods for another hour or so before stopping in a clearing. It took me a moment to realize it was the same one where we'd first met. Somehow, she'd been able to find it again without the map and without appearing to be lost.

"This seemed like a good place to camp tonight, don't you think?" she asked as she moved to the center and began unpacking the tent.

"Yeah, yeah, it is," I replied. After all, it was where our adventure began and today was our last day together. Tomorrow, we'd leave together, I was certain of it. Still, all throughout our dinner, I found myself watching her, looking for some signs of what she was thinking, what she was feeling. Though I was sure she no longer had a desire to die, as we set up camp, I realized it was only in my head. So far, she'd said nothing to the effect at all.

In fact, we hadn't talked about it at all, not since that first day. I'd presumed she had already changed her mind, but if she had, wouldn't she have been ready to leave before now? Wouldn't she have started talking about the future, things she wanted to do? But she hadn't. She'd talked of the past and of me, but never herself, never what the future held. Even when she'd talked of letting go and stepping forward, she hadn't said a word about what that entailed.

I also remembered that when we first met, she hadn't acted anything like someone who was about to take their own life. I couldn't just presume her cheerful demeanor was any sign that she had. So now as we went through our usual motions of eating and getting settled in for her to continue her story, I found myself constantly thinking, constantly wondering if I'd done "it", if I'd found that magical switch that would make her want to live. But how could I when I still didn't even know why she wanted to die?

Despite being abandoned, the way she told the story of her life did not sound like someone who was miserable or regretted it. Indeed, she seemed rightfully proud of her accomplishments and as if she had enjoyed her work dating, her friendship with Chika, and her relationship with Hoji. With my pen and notebook ready, I braced myself to find out what had led her to these woods.

Prodigal Daughter

, Hoji was Yuna's most frequent regular. They went on dates at least once a month, sometimes more. When she turned sixteen, he asked to celebrate her birthday with her. He took her to an extra nice dinner and bought her a gorgeous gown. On her seventeenth birthday, he did the same, and again on the eighteenth. It became just another part of their routine. First Saturday date with sex; if there was another date that month it was because he was super stressed and dealing with some annoying client.

It wasn't that she minded. She enjoyed her time with him, and after so many dates together, she considered him a special friend, if nothing else. Sometimes she found her heart wishing there was more to it, that everything wasn't always with him as a client, she the professional. Even her birthdays were paid dates, not special, personal time spent together. But those were dangerous feelings and she quickly buried them if they appeared.

She realized a long time ago that she had learned more about him from chatting about the past with Chika than from Hoji himself. He talked a lot during her dates, but he was always careful not to reveal anything too personal. While he talked about work a lot, she couldn't tell you the name of his company or the name of a single coworker. She knew what he liked to read and the movies he enjoyed, but nothing of his political or religious views. And while he was driven and aiming to be upper management one day, she had no idea if he wanted a wife or kids at some point to share that accomplishment with him.

Maybe because he was the first, or the one who had helped her when she needed it most, she did consider him special. And even with him paying her to be there, she enjoyed her time with him. He was charming, polite, and educated, he never talked down to her or treated her like she was beneath him despite their different places in the social structure of life. That he was a generous lover certainly didn't hurt either; he was one of the few clients she never had to fake it with. In truth if he'd stopped paying, she'd still see him.

Still, there were times she found herself wondering. With his age and occupation, she'd been surprised he was still unmarried and not even in a serious relationship.

Most of those fields were ones where it was strongly preferred that men be married by their 30s if they wanted to advance, though she never understood why that was considered some form of qualification for upper management. If anything, she'd have thought the hours demanded would have made being single a benefit, as it would mean fewer demands on the employees' time. Not that marriage changed that, men would still work anyway. She wasn't sure if she would ever want such easily discarded things like marriage and family, there seemed little point from the examples she'd seen.

A few months after her eighteenth birthday, Hoji had her meet him at a hotel room. It was an unusual request for him as they usually met at a restaurant first, but she agreed. It was the same hotel and even the same room that he'd gotten her that first night they met. While it seemed almost romantic at first, instead a strange pit formed in her stomach as she knocked on the door. When he let her in, he smiled at her and kissed her cheek, but his touch seemed cooler, more distant.

Rather than lead her to the bed, he led her to a pair of chairs by the window. "Yuna-chan…"

"Yes?" Something told her what he was about to say, but damned if she would make it easier on him.

"This…this will have to be our last meeting together." His voice at least was tinged with regret, even if she doubted if he really had any at all.

"Oh? Okay, then," she replied, keeping her tone purposefully light, nonchalant, as if it didn't bother her in the least.

That seemed to throw him a bit, enough that the mask he'd been wearing slipped and he looked bothered. "The thing is, you know how these things go in business. The higher ups have made it clear that if I want to progress further, I really need to hurry up and get married, that having the right wife is important for being able to do all those business functions and what not they'd expect of me. It's silly, really, but, that's how it goes in these kinds of places."

"So…you're getting married then?"

"Yes. My parents arranged for an omiai. The woman I met, Tomiko, was very nice and we got along well. She will be a good wife, I think."

For a moment, the odd pain knifing through her caused her pride to slip. "Why does that mean we can't see each other anymore? You wouldn't be the first married guy with someone on the side."

"True, and I thought about it, believe me, but well, that would be unfair to her to start our marriage that way. And she really is a good woman. I want to at least try to do right by her. Giving up what little free time I have to spend with you instead of her would be wrong of me. Besides, the higher up I climb, the more my personal life will be subject to scrutiny. Having a mistress is far more understandable than being a client to a…" He broke off, seeming to reconsider whatever word he'd thought about saying.

"I see. I guess that's understandable," Yuna said, burying the pain to examine later. Instead she donned her best acting mask ever to smile at him. "Well, I wish you the best then and I hope you have a good marriage. I must admit, you've always been one of my favorites so I'll miss our time together."

He looked confused again, just like she hoped. "I, yes, as will I. I mean…"

She stood before he could finish and kissed his cheek. "Thank you for telling me, Hoji. I would have hated wondering where you'd gone. Good luck."

Leaving him no time to say more, she made her way to the door and told him goodbye. As accustomed as she was to hiding her true self on her dates, it was easy enough for her to continue smiling as she left the hotel, boarded the train back to her neighborhood, and even stop to say hello to one of her neighbors before letting herself into her apartment.

After taking a quick shower then running a bubble bath, she let herself sink into the warm water before finally letting her tears out. Somehow, somewhere along the way he'd wormed his way into her heart and now he was gone, gone just like everyone else. It wasn't as if she'd really been surprised. Of course she wouldn't even be someone he could consider as a potential wife. If seeing her alone was enough to be a danger to his career, marrying her would have been ten times worse.

But still, as she sat in the tub, hugging her arms around herself, she couldn't help whispering the words she would have never admitted to him. "Why not me? After all this time, why not me? You said I understood you better than anyone, you said I was precious and special to you, you said I meant the world to you. So why not me?"

Until then, she hadn't even realized that she'd been hoping Hoji would want to keep her, to stop being a client and provider and have a real relationship. Angry at herself, she got out of the tub and got ready for bed. She knew better, had seen so many girls heartbroken when a favorite client stopped coming, girls who'd foolishly let themselves believe they were anything more than a warm body and a mindless distraction.

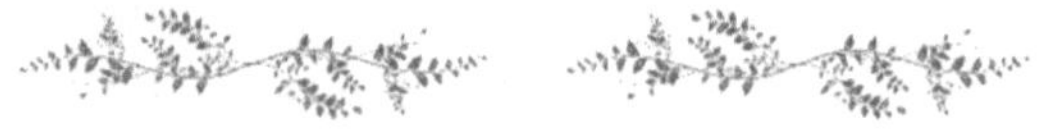

IN THE END, SHE got over Hoji's departure the same as she had the rest in her life, by continuing to walk forward. Though Hoji had been her guarantor, since Yuna had a good established history and was now eighteen, Chika hadn't asked her to leave. She had said a few choice words about the stuff Hoji had said and his sudden pending marriage, though Yuna could have sworn she also looked just a bit sad too. She wrote it off as Chika being disappointed in how her friend had acted, considering she'd known him so long and thought him better than that. Yuna wondered if Chika was also worried he would he dump their friendship the way he had Yuna. Would he see Chika as too low class now that he was moving up in the world? While Yuna got over her own hurt quick enough, she was filled with anger at the thought of him possibly doing that to Chika and hoped he wasn't that foolish.

Fortunately, at that point, Yuna was so well-established that even the loss of Hoji's regular jobs didn't cause more than a minor blip in her finances. She took six to eight clients a week, including one or two sex clients, and continued hoarding her money other than what she had to spend to update her clothes and the like. Her other regulars also helped cover for the gap in Hoji's excessive payments.

Not long after losing Hoji, she finished her high school program and earned her degree. Her teachers at the correspondence school all encouraged her to consider college due to her grades and how well she had done, but she still had no idea what she wanted to do with herself once she had to stop dating, not enough to bother with school. She was certain that whatever she did, she would continue being in business for herself. After all these years working as an entrepreneur, she just couldn't see herself answering to somebody else or having to follow anyone else's rules.

As she flowed from eighteen to nineteen, she realized she was growing bored with dating. Though she acted well enough for her clients to not notice, her heart wasn't in it anymore. She had plenty of savings and could quit anytime she wanted, but some undefinable fear kept her working anyway. Maybe she was just afraid to cut off the regular income without having a plan, she wasn't sure. But with nothing else in mind to do, she just kept doing it, unable to bring herself to leap without looking.

Then, when she was twenty, life decided to give her a push and she found herself homeless again. A careless tenant caused a fire in the building, destroying half the units, including Yuna's. She'd come home from shopping to find firetrucks and smoke everywhere, and Chika crying outside, heartbroken at the loss of her main source of income. Much like Yuna though, Chika picked herself up quickly and started to rebuild. She'd promised Yuna a unit when she was done, at the same rate though it would be bigger and better, but it would be a few months before it would be ready.

Standing outside with the smell of smoke and burnt wood still lingering in the air, Yuna decided to take it as a sign. Just as being dumped on a street corner had brought such a significant change to her life, she was again standing homeless and adrift, but this time she was not without options. Sure, she'd lost almost everything, including the mementos and gifts from her clients over the years, her computer, all her clothes, but she hadn't lost it all. Beyond still being there, she had backups of the computer data and plenty of money in the bank, plus whatever she got from the insurance company for her lost belongings.

Chika had offered to find her a temporary place until the rebuild was done, but Yuna declined. Instead, she figured it was time to do some of the other things she always wanted to do. Sitting in her favorite coffee house with a new notebook and pen, she began making a new list. A list of every dream she'd been denied since her parents had cut her off.

She'd had a few clients who'd treated her to places like Tokyo Disneyland and other big sights, but she'd never seen a lot of the "sights" of Japan. Other than the one trip to London, she hadn't really left the Asian continent before. She tried to think of every place she'd ever read about or seen on TV shows or in a movie that had appealed to her and added them all to her list. There were a lot of activities she would have done during her school years that she missed out on too, so she added those to the list as well.

She let her last remaining regular client, her movie loving friend, Hayate, know that she'd be out of town for a while, exchanging a heartfelt and sincerely regretful goodbye. She also had a tearful goodbye with Chika before she headed off with a small bag of essentials to check things off her list.

Having honed her English skills for clients, she headed to the United States to see the famous Grand Canyon. She shopped the streets of New York and took in a show at Broadway. Rode the train across the country, marveling at the sights while being amused at American's seeming contentedness at having such slow-moving trains.

She went to Paris to scale the Eiffel Tower, Rome to explore the historical city and monuments, Kidepo Valley National Park in Uganda for a true wildlife safari, and even Australia to marvel at the empty vastness of the Outback in person. She took a cruise around South America, getting to see more historical sights while enjoying the unique experiences of "living" on a ship. It was exhausting, but worth every minute of it and every dollar she spent. Though she made sure she didn't pay any more than she should, she also let herself be a little more relaxed with her money, indulging in nicer hotels and a few expensive outings. Perhaps even then, she'd already decided the ultimate goal she was moving towards.

A year and a half later, she returned to Japan, but continued travelling. She headed to all the "must see" places she'd heard about from clients, including the Poroto Kotan Ainu Museum in Shiraoi that a kindly history professor had mentioned while telling her about the plight of the Ainu peoples and the Hiroshima Peace Park that so many of her peers would have gone to during school. She signed up for a class to learn how to go camping, which she'd remembered particularly regretting having to miss out on as a child because Akihito always managed convinced her parents it was bad for her to go. She loved it so much that she took more excursion trips to hone her skills and enjoy the hiking.

Then, at last, she gave in to the masochistic need for closure by returning to her home town of Nagano. Walking around once familiar streets filled her with a mix of nostalgia, regret, and anger. Anger at her family's callous treatment of her, anger at herself for not fighting back, and still, that sad, small, horrible part of her who had never truly gotten over her brother's betrayal.

She walked by her old middle school, a wistful smile touching her lips as she ran her fingers over the closed gate. How different would her life had been had she been allowed to be a child, to be herself all those years? It wasn't that she hated herself now, but some part of her still wished she could meet that young girl, the girl she might have been.

Yuna went to the forest where she'd gone so many times with Noritaka and Akihito, but the old spot was gone, replaced by a large apartment complex, office buildings, and hotels. The forest, it seemed, had gone the way of so many other similar spots, lost to the tides of progress. It was bittersweet, standing roughly where she'd lost her innocence but now surrounded by pavement and cars.

She got turned around a bit, but eventually found her old childhood home. Standing across the street, she wondered if they even were there anymore, the family she'd once loved so much and who she'd foolishly thought loved her. The house looked much like she remembered it, though the paint was more faded and would need a touch up soon.

The door opened and a girl who looked to be six or so came out, bouncing down the path to the gate with a pink backpack on and a gift bag swinging from her hand. It took Yuna a moment to notice a woman standing in the doorway, watching the girl leave.

Her mother looked older, thinner, with grayed hair and clear lines under her eyes even from that distance. "Now, make sure to thank them for having you and to give Emi's mom the cookies right away. Be helpful and polite, okay." As she waved the girl off, Yuna's mom had a kind-looking smile on her face, a smile Yuna couldn't remember ever seeing her make.

"I will, Okasan, I promise. See you tomorrow."

Yuna watched her previously unknown sister skip down the sidewalk, presumably heading out to visit a friend's house overnight for the first time. Her sister…her little sister, doing something she'd never been allowed to do. Part of her wanted to follow, curious about this relative she never knew, but she didn't really feel like a relative or "family", any more than the rest of them did. Too many years had passed for her to feel even a fleeting connection to the little girl passing out of sight.

When Yuna looked back at the house, her mom was still standing in the doorway, only now she was looking across the street, looking at Yuna. It felt as though hours passed as they stood there, before her mother finally turned, walked back inside, and closed the door. As it had been years ago, her family's home was no longer a place for her.

"Goodbye, Mother," Yuna whispered then walked away. She didn't need to see her father, as his reaction would no doubt be the same. So instead she continued walking through the old neighborhood on her way back to the train station.

"Yuna-chan? Is that you?" A woman's voice called out to her from behind her. She turned to find Akihito's old girlfriend, Kira, walking towards her. "It is you!"

Kira embraced her warmly. It was the kind of welcome she wished she'd gotten from her mother, but still Yuna returned the embrace. She'd never had any issues with Kira, who had often taken time to teach her beauty tips when she wasn't making out with Akihito.

"Hi Kira-san. How are you?" Yuna asked as they separated.

"Good, good. Though I'm so ready for this one to drop!" she said pointing to her bulging stomach. "As much as he's moving around, I think he's coming out early."

"Ah, congratulations!"

Kira gave her a long, assessing glance. "It's been so long. I still couldn't believe it when I found out what happened to you. I worried about you, being on your own, but it looks like you managed?"

"I've done okay, yeah. Just finishing up a long period of travel and decided to come here on my way back home. I thought it might be nice to see all the places I remembered from my childhood, you know?"

"Yeah, that can be fun. I went by my old middle school myself when I got pregnant with my first kid. It was nostalgic, but brought back lots of good memories," she said in a wistful tone before her smile faded. "Did you go by your old home?"

Yuna nodded. "I'm still not welcomed there it seems. I did see my little sister for a moment though. I thought about seeing Akihito, but…"

"Do you know where he is?"

"No. I was going to look him up, but then I decided it wouldn't be any point after all these years. It would just open old wounds and dig new ones. I do hope he's happy, though?" she asked despite herself.

"Ah…I…I guess you couldn't know if your family still has you cut off."

"Know what?"

"Come on. He isn't far from here," Kira said as she grabbed her hand. Yuna debated shaking her off, but her expression looked so serious and determined that she followed obediently along until they passed under a familiar entrance into a cemetery. Had her brother become a caretaker there? The truth didn't even occur to her as a possibility until they stood in front of a grave marker bearing their family name. Below it, she spotted Akihito's name, with the year of death listed as the same year she'd been dumped in Shinjuku.

"Akihito…he…" She collapsed to the ground, his name blurred as tears filled her eyes. She reached out towards the stone marker, her hand shaking as she ran her fingers over his name.

Kira squatted down beside her and put her hand on Yuna's shoulder. "I'm sorry."

"Nii-san…how?" Yuna forced herself to ask.

"When your dad left you in Shinjuku, Akihito was really angry at himself for just going to work and leaving you to deal with them by yourself. He told me that he'd just expected them to yell at you though, maybe ground you or something. He never imagined they would do something like that. After your father got back, he thought if he just let them calm down for a few hours they would get over it and go get you. But then they didn't and days passed. Anytime he tried to talk about you, they would cut him off and tell him you were dead as far as they were concerned."

"He always was the golden child. Nii-san could do no wrong, while I was always just an add-on, someone to make him shine brighter," Yuna said, any bitterness over that truth long lost to the passage of time.

"Akihito…he never could see how wrong what he did to you was. To him it was no different than if you'd gotten bad grades or something, just a mistake he could easily smooth over. It never occurred to him that he had serious issues for doing those things to you. But to me, your parents were far worse. To punish you, to blame you…" Kira's voice was tinged with the anger Yuna should have felt. "He worried about you, so much. He cried and said he'd never forgive himself if something happened to you."

"Then why didn't he call me? He had my number! He could have just called. He could have come to get me," Yuna cried.

Kira hugged her tight. "He tried, I swear he tried. He didn't realize your parents had gone into his phone when he wasn't looking and changed his address book. It sent his calls to you to a non-working number. He thought you weren't answering because you were angry at him and hurt at what he'd done. He was desperate to talk to you, to beg forgiveness and bring you back home."

"I tried to call him, but he cut off the call."

"No, that was your parents too. He'd forgotten his phone at the house the day your parents found out, so when you called, they were the ones who answered and cut the call. They then blocked your number and your email address from his phone. He discovered that later, after he got suspicious and finally checked through his phone records. That's when he discovered the issue with the address book too. That was on the fourth day after they'd abandoned you.

"When he discovered what they had done, Akihito went straight home and demanded to know where they took you, where he could find you. He even threatened to move out and cut them off if they didn't let you come back home. That was the only way he was able to find out you'd been left in Shinjuku. It made him even more afraid for you, knowing what that place was like, so he grabbed your father's car keys and ran out of the house, determined to go find you. He called me before he left, asking if he could bring you to my place when he got back."

Kira's voice trailed off and she gave Yuna another squeeze. "He was so distraught, and it was late and he'd never been a very good driver. The police said he was speeding and lost control of the car in the Joshin-etsu tunnel through Saijo Mountain. They estimated he was going 150 kilometers per hour. He crashed into the wall, then his car bounced off it and into the opposite wall. It was a miracle his car didn't crash into anyone else. They believe the impact on the first wall killed him instantly."

Yuna's grief overwhelmed her and she barely heard the last bit. After all that time, thinking he'd forgotten her, to learn that Akihito had been coming for her and in doing so had gotten himself killed. Her wails and sobs shook her body as Kira held her tight, whispering random comforting sounds that had little effect on easing her pain. Of course her mother hadn't welcomed her; in their minds she had taken their precious son away.

"I'm sorry, I'm sorry..." Yuna said as she sat up and

tried to get her tears under control, before she dampened Kira's shirt anymore. "I just...I never imagined...I thought he'd abandoned me...I..."

"No, it's okay. I should apologize. I should have broken the news more gently." Kira looked at her worriedly. "Are you going to be okay?"

"Yes, yes, I will. Sorry, I guess I had more feelings about everything still inside me than I thought." Yuna tried ease the older girl's concerns. As she wiped her face again, she noticed the name carved beside her brother's. "Father?"

Kira nodded. "On the day of Akihito's funeral, someone asked about you, about why you weren't there. Your father flew into such a rage he had a heart attack. He survived, but he was changed after that. Then your mom had your little sister and for a while it seemed like they would be okay, but then he had another heart attack two years ago and never recovered."

The news of her father's death hurt far less than Akihito's; she was sad to learn he'd died, but it didn't make her heart ache the way it was aching now over her brother.

"Um, Kira-san...my little sister, does Mom love her?"

"Yeah. Sad as it is, I think they did learn from their mistakes. She takes good care of her and dotes on her, but she doesn't spoil her the way they did Akihito. I've talked to her a few times and she's growing up to be a pretty good kid. Smart as a whip and a good head on her shoulders."

Yuna sighed with relief. "That's good. That should be okay then. I'd hate if she was living like I did, but yeah, she did look happy."

"So, what will you do now? How long are you in town for?"

"Oh, I'm just here for the day." Yuna said, having decided it right then. "I should probably go soon to catch my train back home. It's been awhile since I've been back."

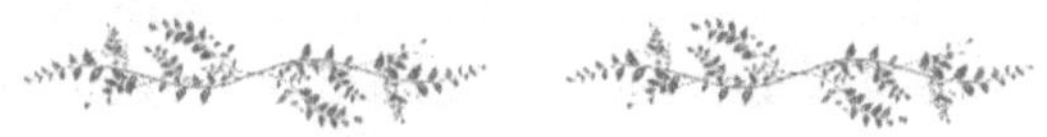

YUNA ARRIVED BACK IN Shinjuku in the early evening and headed for Chika's place where her new apartment was waiting. After working out her pain on the train ride home, she was now excited, happy to reunite with her friend and to get settled into her new place. While she could afford the best furniture, she intended to go right back to Dahj's place. It was used, but she liked the styles and it would feel more like the home she knew. She just wasn't into the shiny new look.

But when she arrived, Chika was standing in the door of her apartment in a scandalously passionate embrace with a man. Well, scandalous to anyone who cared about society's views, but Chika hadn't, and for a moment, Yuna was happy that her friend had found someone.

That was before she recognized that back, that hair, that embrace. It was Hoji, Hoji whose tongue was down Chika's throat and looking for all the world like he wanted to take her inside and fuck her. Her Hoji, who couldn't marry a commoner or risk even being in an affair with one, was now making out in the open with someone just like her.

Yuna stood there, mute, watching them. Her bag almost fell off her shoulder, but she managed to rouse herself enough to catch it. She was tempted to turn and run away, but she'd always hated those kinds of scenes in movies and manga. Not that she thought it would turn out to be a stereotypical understanding, there was no mistaking the kiss for trying to get dust out of her eye or her hair caught on his jacket or some other equally silly set up. No, Yuna realized she had clearly been blind to a few things these last few years.

Turning on her best smile, she straightened her bag and walked towards them as if completely unbothered by the sight. It was Chika who spotted her first; her eyes went wide with shock as she partially shoved Hoji away and stumbled on her name. Hoji turned and had the decency to try to look at least somewhat ashamed, though the look failed with the lipstick all on his lips.

"Yuna, I—"

She cut him off with a cold look. "I'm here to see Chika, not you, so just stay quiet like a good fellow, will you."

Chika had tears streaming down her face. "I swear, Yunie, it started after you left to travel. There was never anything before. I mean, yeah, I had a crush on him in high school, but I thought you two would end up together. And then he came to dump me like he dumped you and we fought and well, the idiot finally realized he loved me, and I know I should have talked to you first and told you, I was going to tell you in person and…"

"What about that other girl? Don't tell me you are letting him make you a side piece."

"Hey—" Hoji tried to object, but they both yelled at him to stay out of it.

"No way, I wouldn't have settled for that crap. He broke it off with that other girl and he asked me to marry him." As she swiped at her eyes, Yuna spotted the large diamond sparkling from her finger. It finally clicked, the sad looks she'd kept spotting on Chika's face the night they'd gotten drunk and bashed Hoji for dumping Yuna. It wasn't sorrow for Yuna, but losing her longtime crush.

Yuna gave Chika a hug. "Congratulations. I hope you will both be very happy together."

"I'm sorry, I'm so sorry."

"Don't be. He was just a client, he was your crush. As long as you're happy, that's what matters," Yuna lied with that same bright smile, holding Chika's hands and acting for all the world as if she was happy for her, while thoroughly dismissing Hoji.

"Thank you, Yunie, thank you." It was the pet name Chika had given her, and Yuna hated it at that moment, but she was in full acting mode and smiled along as if everything was great. The last thing she would ever do would be to let these two know how much they had hurt her. "Um, did you want to see the apartment? It's all ready, just like we said."

"Actually, no, I just came to let you know that I decided I enjoyed the traveling so much these last two years that I decided to keep doing it awhile longer. I even found some places I loved so much I am debating moving to one of them, though nothing set in stone yet. For now, I just wanted to stop by while I was in the area to say thank you for the years I got to live here, and so you would know it was okay to stop holding the apartment for me."

"Oh, I, um, okay." Chika's shock was obvious as just last week they had talked about the apartment and excitedly discussing decorating. Yuna had even acted as a sounding board to Chika's proposed new rental rates, since the rebuilds were newer and more modern.

"Anyway, I need to get going, have a train to catch. Thank you again, Chika, and goodbye." Yuna turned and walked away without ever once glancing at Hoji again. She thought she heard him call her name, but she didn't turn back to check. Instead, she continued to the train station, then headed to Shinjuku, revisiting her old stomping grounds. After that, she headed to the love hotel that had been her favorite sleeping spot before she'd gotten the apartment. Even after seven years, she managed to get the same room. It seemed like the perfect full circle to it all, the same place she'd made her first big plans would be the one where she'd make her last ones.

Present

"IN THAT HOTEL ROOM, I thought for a long time about what I wanted to do next. That was when I realized there wasn't anything. That I had done all I really wanted," she finished.

"And, that's when you decided to come here?"

She nodded and looked up at me. "What's the point, really? I mean to live without any rhyme or reason? Going day to day just existing, not really living, because people think you should?"

"But surely there are still things you haven't seen yet? As much as you seem to enjoy exploring and hiking?" I said, trying to keep my own desperation at bay as the tone of her voice made it sound as if she still intended to die tomorrow.

"Oh, there was lots I didn't see, but I don't really have an overwhelming need or desire to see them. Just as I'm sure there is a lot I could do, but that doesn't mean I have a deep desire to actually do them. I mean, have you ever gone out and been a garbage man?"

"Um, no?"

"And you wouldn't want to, right?"

"Well, no," I replied, getting her point. Doing stuff just to do it was meaningless. "So, then you never did find a career or job that interested you? I mean, after you stopped doing enjo kōsai?"

Her head moved side to side. "Nope. And really, what could I do? I wasn't just some high school girl playing around with it, doing just one or two dates. I went on hundreds of dates, maybe even thousands. It isn't the sort of past that is easily ignored by potential employers."

"But you can use a computer! I mean that's an amazing skill in and of itself. I bet some places would overlook your past just to get someone who could, it's a highly desired skill these days and very few people can do it here since not many people use computers in Japan."

"Sorry, but office work sounds so boring. I have no desire to teach or do sales or any of that. I'd rather run my own company, but I have nothing left to sell or skills outside dating, and I'm too old."

"What about hiking?"

"Huh?" She looked at me in confusion. "I do it for fun, but..."

"You could do that as a job too. Some of the hikes you went on were guided, right? You could open your own guide service, do hikes in Japan or around the world. I mean, it's an idea, right? Then you wouldn't have to care who found out because it isn't relevant and no one can fire you if you're your own boss. And the way you can navigate around on memory is fantastic, you'd make a phenomenal guide!" I went on and on, the idea building inside me. I knew she was smart enough to do it, to make a successful business even without a college education, but did it appeal to her? I had no idea, I just kept saying whatever came to mind as I tried to give her some hope, some desire to stay alive.

"Adachi…" She lightly pressed her fingers to my lips, silencing me, before kissing me tenderly. "That's it…that's all of my story that there is to tell."

"So tomorrow?"

A smile fleetingly passed her lips. "Will be tomorrow and we will see what it will bring then. Kiss me, Adachi, I'm cold."

I should have refused, should have demanded we kept talking about tomorrow, kept arguing until she changed her mind, but those eyes and that soft voice were like the most addictive drug I ever knew. Without another word, I cupped her face in my hands and kissed her, then gently pushed her down and claimed her as I had almost every night since we met. That night she was insatiable, relentless in her need for more and more. By the time she finally was satisfied, I could barely move, only hold her with aching arms as she snuggled into my chest.

Before I fell asleep, she whispered my name again. "Hmm?" I replied, forcing myself to stay awake a moment longer.

"Do you think you'll go back tomorrow?"

"Well yeah, I mean, why wouldn't I?"

She gave a slight shrug. "When we first met, it seemed

like you really had come here to die too, to die where they died, to make up for your perceived crimes. Now though, you seem okay, but I just wanted to be sure."

"I…" My denial died in my throat. Had that really been why I came? Had it been in the back of my mind, to end my own life where they had died? And had Yuna really seen that desire that even I hadn't realized was there and that was why she let me come with her? "Is that why you offered me the deal?"

When no reply came, I looked down at her, but her chest rose and fell in the steady rhythm of sleep. Softly, I kissed the top of her head. If she truly had saved my life, then now it was more important than ever that I save hers tomorrow, no matter what it took.

The Final Day

WHEN I AWOKE IN the morning, I was cold despite the thick sleeping bag I was wrapped in. I realized almost immediately that something was missing, that there was no soft, warm body nestled against mine. I bolted up in the tent and turned on the light, as if she'd somehow hidden herself in the small tent we'd been sharing.

Throwing on my clothes, I went outside and looked around, shining my flashlight in a circle around our camp site, looking for her, hoping against hope that she'd just gone to the bathroom and would be walking towards me, laughing at my overreaction.

But there was nothing, not any sign she'd ever been there at all, other than the tent and sleeping bag. Nothing but silence and stillness surrounded me. Giving in to my growing sense of panic, I called her name over and over again, until finally my throat was hoarse. No reply came back. She was gone. Yuna had slipped out of my arms and into the night. I returned to the tent, planning to pack up and go look for her.

Once I was back inside, I realized her backpack was gone and grew disgusted with myself for managing to sleep so soundly that I not only hadn't noticed her leaving but even dragging that back outside and taking it with her. I gathered up the sleeping bag to pack it, having no intention of waiting until it was light enough out to begin searching for her when I spotted it, a sheet of white paper where she used to lay. The bag slipped from my fingers and I picked it up.

Adachi,

I'm sorry I am cheating a little by leaving you before the agreed upon time and by slipping you a sleeping pill so you wouldn't wake up.

To make it up, I'll answer your last question: yes, I offered you the deal because I was afraid if I left you, you would walk the same path I'd come there to walk, and you seemed too nice to be lost to the world just yet.

I'm glad to see you will be okay now. I know I can trust you to tell my story the way the best way it could be.

Thank you for giving me so much of yourself this last week and for listening to my story. I'm so very glad I met you and I hope you have been able to forgive yourself for what happened.

Go back to your paper with your head high and continue your quest for the truth, I know you can get past this and come out a much better reporter for it.

Take care of yourself. I'll never forget our time together.

Until we meet again,

Aiko

P. S. Yuna is the name I used when I worked, so it's what everyone called me after that, but Kurohiko Aiko is my real name, the one my family called me before my first rebirth.

After reading the note again, I carefully folded it and tucked it into my notebook. Then I packed up her sleeping bag and tent and my own things. With the tent light hooked to my belt and my flashlight shining the way, I looked for any sign of which way she might have gone and set out in search of her. I called her name regularly, but I wasn't terribly surprised there was no reply. But still, I continued on until long after the sun came up.

I finally realized it was futile and made my way back to the path around noon. As soon as I was back to my car, I grabbed my phone, but the battery was long dead. I stowed away the stuff in my car and plugged the phone charger in so I could call out. The authorities listened sympathetically as I told them as briefly as possible of the girl I met and that I was concerned she was still in the woods and intended to die. They promised to keep an eye out for her and let the rangers in the park know where she'd last been seen, but there was little else they could do beyond that.

Hoping perhaps she would come out on her own, I stayed there until the entrances were closed for the night. No other car in the parking lot had been there when I'd first gotten there, so I wasn't sure if she'd driven and had left or if she'd walked there. I hated not knowing if she was still there somewhere, now without a tent or sleeping bag to keep her warm. Was she even now in there somewhere dead, her vivaciousness snuffed out by her sense of loss and loneliness, or had our time together somehow changed her, helped her find a new reason to live, and she had simply left on her own for some reason?

In the end, I returned home. Staying there and waiting for word would do nothing for her or for myself. I kept her note on my bedside table, reading it nightly. I met with my editor, Kido, who sounded happy to hear from me. Over beers, I told him of my meeting with Yuna/Aiko and that I wished to tell her story, as I had promised.

"Mmm...I think you should, Adachi-kun, for both

your sakes. I was worried, you know, when you said you were going there, that you had no intention of coming back. You looked broken and defeated and it scared me. But now, now you seem like the Adachi I first meet years ago, eager, ready to tell the world the stories it needs, but now tempered with experience. This, this is good, I think. You'll be okay now, I'm sure of it." He replied in an encouraging tone.

"The one thing I'm not sure of is how to tell it? I mean, there is so much here," I said holding up my notebook, "and I wouldn't want to leave any of it out. It would take a long series of articles to even cover part of it and it might be 'too much' for our sensitive readers."

"Write a book."

"A book?" I hadn't really considered it, but now that he said it, I knew that was the only way I could really tell it properly, in book form rather than as a bunch of articles that people might skip or miss. "You're right…that's what I need to do."

I took another two weeks off at the paper, with Kido's blessing. I traveled to Nagano and Shinjuku to research the rest of Yuna's past (I still couldn't think of her as Aiko). Akihito's accident had been covered by the local news, making it easier to find the rest of the family. With that, I was able to confirm everything she'd told me about her family, including meeting her mother, who only spoke to me briefly and with lingering bitterness over her forgotten daughter. I stood over her brother's grave, barely able to contain myself from cursing his name.

I met Kira-san, now with her second child in tow, who'd filled me in on some of the things about Yuna's brother that Yuna had only been able to guess at. I even found Chika, happily married to Hoji and pregnant with their first child, but also still filled with regret over how things had ended. She'd asked so hopefully if Yuna was happy and doing well that I lied, much as Yuna had in wishing them happiness, and assured her she was.

It wasn't as if I disbelieved her story, for I felt it was the total truth, but I knew she would have teased me if I hadn't backed up her story with proper fact checking. I wasn't about to repeat my past mistakes again. It also aided me in being able to describe the places she'd gone and seen. I even found that crazy love hotel room she'd mentioned so fondly, sleeping in the same bed she'd once slept in, praying desperately that somewhere she was still alive and living a happy life.

After my research time was up, I returned to work, now back to working in the human-interest section, where I could enjoy my work again. At night, I'd go to Shinji's restaurant to work on Yuna's story, using my notes, interviews, and photographs to weave together this tale. And now it is done, and I can only hope I did it, and her, the justice she deserved.

The authorities regularly go through the Aokigahara Forest in search of those who ended their lives there. With every sweep and every body found, I check to see if she is among them, but she never is. I kept her tent and sleeping bag with me and a picture of her Chika gave me, smiling that smile I'd grown to love so much.

I continue to walk forward, moving past my mistakes and working hard not to repeat them. Every morning I wake up, grateful for the life she returned to me, the one I had unknowingly been ready to throw away.

And still, I cannot forget her, the smiling girl I met in

the forest, and I keep hoping one day, we'll find each other again.

Thank you for reading her story,

Tsuguru Adachi

Author's Note

At Week's End, once known as *Girl in the Forest*, is perhaps the hardest novel I've ever written. The initial draft took little time at all, but the revision process was derailed by personal matters, including the death of my beloved mother to illness, and then a few months later, my older brother's death from suicide. My spirit was broken by these events, causing my own mental health to reach a crisis point. It's been a long road back to a healthy state, and I still have a few bits to go, but the good days now far outnumber the bad, and that is a significant step forward.

This novel is set in the Aokigahara Forest, also known as the Sea of Trees. This beautiful ecological and geological wonder is no ordinary forest. Preternatural quiet, lush in foliage with almost no wildlife, grown within volcanic rock and filled with caves and places to explore, it is a beautiful, unnerving spot.

Alas, it also has a far more morbid and heartbreaking reputation, for it is considered to be the second most common place in the world for people to commit suicide, behind the Golden Gate Bridge in San Francisco. There are many theories as to why it gained that reputation, some based in historical superstitions and old beliefs caused by its unusual nature, others blaming more recent media calling attention to the forest's reputation.

The latter made me seriously consider whether it was appropriate to even write a book set in this forest, but for Adachi and Yuna, it was the only place their story could be told. I only hope that in my writing of this book, I was able to show not just the forest's more unsavory views, but also highlight its wonder, beauty, and sights to be seen.

I have the greatest respect and empathy for the sweeper

teams whose job it is to find those who have died in the forest, recover the bodies, and inform their families. Japan, even worse than the United States, still has a long away to go in dealing with the stigma of mental illness and in treating rather than shunning or poo-pooing those who suffer from depression, bipolar disorder, and any other illness. For make no mistake, they are not choices; they are sicknesses, same as the flu, a heart condition, or even cancer. They are diseases of the brain, poorly understood, but there none the less.

I should also clarify this story is in no way intended to be an apologist piece for child molesters of any age. Akihito and Noritaka's actions with Yuna are reprehensible and should have been punished to the full extent of the law. Rather, Yuna's views and reactions to that abuse, particularly as a child, are intended to highlight another side of the abuse.

I personally know several childhood abuse victims who feel like they cannot talk about their stories because they do not fit the narrative, i.e., they weren't crying and screaming the whole time, or in agony and miserable. Rather they, like Yuna, simply didn't realize they were being abused or hurt, because it caused no physical pain and they trusted their abusers. Far more abusers get away with it just for that reason because they are skilled at not harming their charges physically while also psychologically manipulating them into thinking it's all okay.

In this way, I wanted to give representation to the other victims, the ones still struggling between "knowing" it was wrong and abuse, but having no actual "bad" memories of the abuser and so they second guess whether it really was abuse or if they were somehow to blame. We need to shift the narrative away from just "it must have hurt" and focus on the fact that an adult or near adult deliberately manipulated a child for sexual purposes. Just as with rape, the lack of force or pain does not make it "okay" or lesser than violent penetration.

I thank you for reading *At Week's End*, and I hope no matter what life may be throwing at you, that you too can continue walking forward one step at a time.

Sherelle

Thank You for Reading!

Want to know when my next novel is coming out? Head to my website, SherelleWinters.com and get a free novelette as well!

Also by Sherelle Winters

Aisuru

Deviations

Broken Wing

www.ingramcontent.com/pod-product-compliance
Lightning Source LLC
Chambersburg PA
CBHW061436210726

48287CB00007B/2236